DEATH ON THE CAUSEWAY

Also by Caleb Wygal

Mytle Beach Mystery Novels
The Brass Key (Short Story Prequel)
Death on the Boardwalk
Death Washes Ashore
Death on the Golden Mile

Lucas Caine Novels
Moment of Impact
A Murder in Concord
Blackbeard's Lost Treasure
The Search for the Fountain of Youth

DEATH ON THE CAUSEWAY

A MYRTLE BEACH MYSTERY

CALEB WYGAL

FRANKLIN/KERR
KANNAPOLIS, NORTH CAROLINA

Published by Franklin/Kerr Press
1040 Dale Earnhardt Blvd. #185
Kannapolis, North Carolina 28083
www.FranklinKerr.com

Edited by Lisa Borne Graves
Cover photo by Dave Gombka
Cover art and design by Mibl Art
Author photo by Pamela Hartle
Interior design by Jordon Greene

Printed in the United States of America

FIRST EDITION

Hardback ISBN 978-0-578-31315-3
Paperback ISBN 979-8-9860006-9-5

Fiction: Cozy Mystery
Fiction: Amateur Sleuth
Fiction: Southern Fiction

For my older sister, Betsy.
Thanks for the support and encouragement
through everything.

CHAPTER
ONE

Life has a habit of changing when you least expect it, and on this most normal of days, it happened again.

Months had passed with no sign of Autumn's phone. Life had gone on. It had to. I had no choice. As much as I would have liked to throw all my responsibilities aside and get to the bottom of Autumn's death, I couldn't. People depended on me.

My first solo book was released by my publisher in early February, and soon I was getting invited to book signings and speaking engagements. The book went over well with readers better than expected. They were already asking when the next book in the series was going to be released. I had a few ideas knocking around the inside of my head and scrawled on napkins from the bookstore. To this point, I hadn't written the first word of the next book. Maybe after Memorial Day.

Currently, I was stuck in molasses-slow Memorial Day weekend traffic moving through Conway on 501. The unofficial start of summer brought tourists from all over the country to the Grand Strand, happy to get away from home after months of being pent up in their homes for the winter and spring. With the weather warming and kids getting out of school, families were eager to spend three days in the Grand Strand. Many of them did not know where they were going, even with GPS, and it caused headaches for us locals. Not to mention the authorities. The police and fire departments spent a large amount of time and resources cleaning up after fender-benders.

Conway was a chokepoint for much of the traffic flowing into town. I was on my way home from an author event for the library in Marion, sitting at a stoplight. I'd met some new readers, signed a few books, and enjoyed a tasteful charcuterie spread. It had been a good day, but I was looking forward to getting home. My plan was to grab a chicken biscuit from a Bojangles on 544 on the way back to my home in Surfside Beach. I didn't feel like getting home, lugging cases of books back inside my house, and then making dinner.

It was days like this when I missed Autumn. If one of us was going to get home late, the other had made sure dinner was waiting. I had wound up doing most of the cooking, but it had been my pleasure. I liked to cook, and she'd worked hard at her job. She had received a small inheritance from a rich uncle that enabled us to open Myrtle Beach Reads together. I managed the bookstore while she kept her job at the courthouse. Her intention had been to do that until the store made enough money to where she could cut back on the number of hours she would work and eventually quit.

She never made it to that goal.

It's been three years since her death. One year since Detective Gomez told me her suspicion that Autumn might have been murdered rather than having died of a heart attack at her desk at the courthouse. My life has changed in several ways since that night. The night I, your average everyday bookstore owner and coffee-slinger, Clark Thomas, solved the murder of Paige

Whitaker. The first of four murders I'd solved.

Since then, I tried to figure out *if* Autumn had been murdered, and if so, who might have done it and how? I had come across her phone in my desk, charged it, and found several threatening text messages from an unknown number. Gomez had a tech person who could try to get more from the phone. I'd handed her the phone and never saw it again. Someone had stolen it from the forensics lab.

Gomez said the tech had put the phone in a tray and placed it into an evidence cabinet. The tech hadn't told anyone about the phone. I had thanked Gomez for helping, and she'd said she would let me know if she learned anything further. That was eight months ago.

Haven't heard a peep.

Only four people knew about the phone. Myself, the tech, Gomez, and her partner, Detective Moody. Its theft kept me up late ever since, racking my brain, trying to figure out who would steal the phone and how they could have known about it. The mystery behind the person who sent Autumn the threatening messages continued.

My Jeep rolled to a stop at another light. This was one of those days where I hit every light. Hurry up and stop. Traffic was bumper-to-bumper, as was typical in Conway this time of year. The temperature on the dash approached ninety, while the sun in the rearview fell to the horizon. I cranked the AC to high.

I tapped my thumbs on the steering wheel to a Pearl Jam song I'd listened to as a teen, now on the classic rock station. That made me feel old. It wasn't the first time I've heard some of my favorite music growing up on 104.1. Part of life, I guess. At least they considered it classic and didn't confine the song to the trash can.

To my left was a family in a minivan. The windows in the back were tinted, but I saw several shadows moving about. The mom was in the front passenger seat, head back, staring at a cell phone. The dad's head poked forward, trying to see the street signs, making sure they were on the right track.

To my right was a mobile home sales lot. Several doublewides in various configurations dotted the lot. The small sales office in the center had a "Closed" sign on the door. Two mobile homes sat side-by-side on this end of the lot, with the ends of the houses facing the road. There was, perhaps, seven feet of space separating the two homes.

In between them, halfway down their length, was a petite blonde-haired woman. I might not have looked twice, except for two things. One, she looked like a California girl in a Carolina town. Two, she stomped her heels into the gravel lot as she screamed into a cell phone.

And she would change my life. Again.

CHAPTER
TWO

I couldn't take my eyes off her. She wore a low-cut green blouse, navy skirt, and heels. Her hair fell past her shoulders. It glowed, even in the shadows between the mobile homes.

The stoplight remained red. She yelled, gesticulated, banged a hand on the vinyl siding of one home, then hung up the phone with an angry jab on the screen. She looked at the sky and raised her hands, as though asking for help. Then she took two steps and sat down on the temporary wood stairs leading to the front door.

The car behind me honked, breaking my trance. I looked up and saw the light had turned green. The van beside me was now inching through the intersection as I remained stationary. I glanced in the rearview. An older woman in the Mercedes behind me blew her horn. Guess she was in a hurry to stop at the next intersection if the traffic pattern for the last half hour held. I stuck my hand out the window and gave her a sarcastic thumbs up.

I made a snap decision and turned on the blinker and turned right and then made another quick right into the mobile home seller's gravel lot. Rocks crunched underneath wide tires. Plumes of dust arose. The doublewide was cream-colored. I parked and turned the car off. Eddie Vedder's voice died away.

After snatching the keys from the ignition, I opened the door. The homes for sale between the Jeep and 501 muffled passing traffic. The girl never looked up from the stoop.

Taking a deep breath, I stepped around the Jeep and approached her through the alley between homes. I cleared my throat, hoping she would notice me. She didn't.

When I was within hand's reach, I stopped. Her head was down between folded arms atop her knees. She sobbed to herself.

"Excuse me," I said. "Is everything okay?"

If my approach surprised her, she didn't show it. She looked up with mascara smeared across her cheeks. Dangling earrings shook. An elegant jawline framed thin lips and a button nose. She tucked a blonde strand behind her ear to get a better view of me. The California girl vibe I had at first glance melted away. A true Cali girl would have worn waterproof mascara or had fake eyelashes. This girl, and I do mean girl, did not fit that mold. She couldn't have been older than her mid-twenties.

For once, I wasn't dressed in shorts and a Hawaiian shirt with flip-flops. I had dressed a little more respectable for the author event: khakis, white oxford button-down, and blue Sperrys. Even my face was smooth from a good shave before leaving.

She sniffled. "No. It's not."

"Is there anything I can do to help you?"

I reached into my pocket, pulled out an unused tissue, and handed it to her.

She accepted it with a soft "Thank you," and blew her nose once, then folded the tissue over and gave it another go.

I realized it might help to broker trust rather than be some random dude who showed up unexpectedly between two homes in a vacant mobile home lot. "I was sitting over there, waiting at the stoplight, when I saw you on the phone before hanging up. I didn't see a car nearby, so I figured you were stranded or something and might need help."

"That's a good way of putting it. Stranded. I'm a thousand miles from home and have no idea where my fiancé, Brian, is." Her voice was soft and carried a slight accent. Definitely not a Cali girl.

"Was that him you were talking to on the phone?"

"No. That was the police. I told them Brian was missing."

"What did they say?"

"That there wasn't much they could do until he'd been gone for a day or so. Unless he was a danger to himself. Or others."

The protocols surrounding missing persons were familiar to me in only what I had read in books or on TV. What she said came as no surprise. "Is he? A danger to himself or others, that is."

She snorted. I wasn't sure if she was clearing the snot from her nose or trying to muster a laugh. The latter, I hoped. My hope proved true.

"Brian? A danger? Pfft. A danger to all-you-can-eat buffets maybe, but not to himself or others."

"That's good, I guess."

"They said I had to wait twenty-four hours before I could file a missing-persons report. I told them he took our camper van and stranded me here."

"And you were upset that they couldn't help you."

"Yeah, that and stupid Brian. I gave them my name and number and information about him. Like a description and birthdate. They told me to get an Uber and suggested a few motels."

"That's about as helpful as you'll get on a weekend like this.

How long ago did he leave you?"

"He's been gone about an hour. We were at a coffee place one street over. I went to the bathroom. When I came out, he was gone. His phone goes straight to voicemail."

"Did he say he was going somewhere? Did you have some place you needed to be?"

"He didn't. We just finished filming a review at The Trestle Restaurant and were headed back to the campground."

"Which campground?"

"PirateLand on the lower end of Myrtle Beach."

"Gotcha. Are you all food reviewers or something?"

She sat up. The flow of conversation seemed to have comforted her to a degree.

"Yeah. We call ourselves the 2 Foodie Nomads. We travel the country in a little camper van, finding cool places to do reviews."

"Like Guy Fieri on Diners, Drive-Ins, and Dives?"

"Yeah, kinda like that. Brian idolizes him. Doing this is what Brian wanted to do."

"And you went along for the ride?"

Her eyes lit. She smiled for the first time. It was cute. "Yeah, you could say that."

The sun crept lower. The shadows between the mobile homes stretched. Daylight was wasting.

I repeated my initial question. "Is there anything I can do to help you?"

She gave me an empty look and shook her head from side to side. "I don't know. I kept hoping he'd come back."

"Do you have any friends or family nearby?"

"Not for a thousand miles."

"Right. You mentioned that." I tightened my jaw. "Where

are you going to stay tonight if he doesn't come back?"

She shook her head. "I dunno. Can't very well go to PirateLand without the camper van. We were getting ready to head south to Charleston on Tuesday."

"Do you have any money on you?"

She looked up at me and leaned away, wrapping her arms around her pocketbook.

I held up a pleading hand. "No, don't get me wrong. I have no intention of robbing you. I'm just trying to figure out what kind of help you need, and money is part of it. I didn't know if your fiancé ran off with your money too, or what."

The death grip loosened on the pocketbook. She let out a breath. "I have most of that. We have a joint account, but he only carries cash. He closed his checking and savings accounts down before we hit the road. I added him to mine, but he doesn't use it."

"Does he carry a debit card?"

"He does but doesn't use it."

"You could monitor your checking account and see if he uses it."

She sat up and stared at the siding of the cream-colored mobile home in front of her as my implication sunk in. Tears welled. "Are you suggesting that he's not coming back? That he's leaving me?"

I tilted my head. "I wouldn't put it out of the realm of possibility. He waited until you couldn't see him to leave. Turned his phone off. Has he done anything like this before?"

"No. Never." She stood and looked at the sky. "What am I going to do?"

The humidity caused my shirt to stick to me. I sweated all over. She glistened. I wanted to get back in the Jeep and air conditioning. As I watched her standing there, touching the base of her neck with one hand and staring at a point in the gravel off to the side, I decided there was only one reasonable thing to do.

"Come on," I said. "Hop in the Jeep. Let's try to figure this out."

CHAPTER
THREE

My mom taught me to never accept rides from strangers. That didn't stop Shelly from climbing into the passenger seat of the Jeep. Our brief and sweaty initial encounter gave her enough trust in me to ride along. She may have had reservations, but after speaking with the police dispatch and getting their advice, a ride with me was more appealing than with an anonymous Uber driver.

I got back on 501 and drove into an immediate traffic jam. The vehicles in front of me had their blinkers on, trying to get into the left lane. After driving a few hundred yards, the reason became obvious. A fender-bender between a Kia SUV with Wisconsin tags and a local Chevy SUV was the culprit. A billboard for a well-known accident attorney loomed over their heads, urging anyone in an accident to dial all 4s. He had advertisements all over the area, so there was a good chance the out-of-towners would learn about him at some point. If they hadn't already. If not him, then there would be another equally renowned attorney telling you to dial all 2s. Passive ambulance chasers.

Shelly had been quiet after we hit the road. She gazed out the passenger window, twirling a lock of hair with one hand and rubbing the other up and down her thigh.

"Typical Memorial Day weekend traffic," I said, breaking the silence. "Tourists stream into town, traveling for hours in a hurry to get here, and get into accidents ten miles from their destination."

"They say most car accidents happen within a mile of a person's home," Shelly said.

"Not here."

She turned to me. "I don't know where we're going or what I'm supposed to do, but I can't thank you enough for stopping to help."

"Don't mention it. I hope someone else would have seen you and come along."

Her lips formed a cute grimace. "Yes, but I don't know what their intentions might have been. You seem like a nice and trustworthy enough person."

"Thanks, I think."

"What would you suggest I do?"

I turned my attention to the road in front of us. Her situation piqued my curiosity. Why would Brian strand the woman he loves here and now? I needed to learn more.

"I know a few people, women I trust, who you might stay with tonight if we don't find your beloved."

Her shoulders sagged in relief. I wasn't about to suggest that the pretty girl stay with me. She might jump out of the Jeep at the next stoplight if I did, and I wouldn't blame her. If it weren't for Marilyn, Karen, Margaret, and Winona, I would offer to put her up for the night in a motel.

"Let's hope we do, and we learn that there's a reasonable explanation for all of this," she said with conviction.

I wasn't so convinced. "Tell me about you and Brian."

"Where to start?" she said, settling into her seat. "We grew up together in a little suburb north of Baton Rouge named Ethel. My parents owned a farm where people could come and pick their own raspberries, blueberries, and blackberries."

"Sounds scrumptious."

A half-smile formed, perhaps as she thought of a pleasant memory of growing up on the farm. "Mom and Grandma baked the best pies from those berries."

"I'm sure. What about Brian?"

"His parents own a chain of restaurants in central and northern Louisiana named Gator's Landing."

"I've been to New Orleans once, but don't remember it," I said.

"It's easy to get lost in the shuffle of food places there."

"That's the truth."

She flicked a hand. "Their place was like Applebee's, but they also serve gator."

"I had that once," I said. "I bought an alligator smoked sausage from the French Market in New Orleans. It was good."

"It is. Anyway, we were high school sweethearts and went to college together. He's an only child. His dad runs the business but is having health problems. He's going to hand over control of the day-to-day operations to Brian after we finish our foodie tour. He's worked with his dad and the business since he was young and is quite good at it, from what I can tell."

"Is his dad dying?"

"No. The stress of the job is getting to him. He had a major heart attack, followed by a triple bypass. He went back to the office the following week and worked harder than ever. Brian's mom convinced his dad to take a step back. He agreed, but first

Brian wanted to do something on his own."

"Travel the country, reviewing restaurants?"

"Yes. Brian has all this knowledge of how the industry works. Even being around it every day, it still fascinates him to see what other chefs come up with and how their mind works. He can cook, but he's not a trained chef."

"What did he go to college for?"

"Restaurant management."

"What did you do?"

"I got a degree in English. I write. I blog. I run our YouTube channel, social media, and website. He's the on-camera expert. I sit there, look pretty, and provide my two cents when I can. We've been successful. We have enough of a following that we make a little money off it."

"Is that how you finance it?"

She shook her head. "No, Brian's dad paid for everything. He urged Brian to have his own adventure before stepping into the family business. He may not have been healthy, but he understood what he was asking his son to do."

"What about you?"

"I support him in all he does. He's done a lot for me through the years." Her voice broke. "I love him so much."

I reached over and patted her shoulder. Consoling people was a foreign language to me. I didn't know what to do. In situations like this, I asked myself what Detective Gomez would say. I met her after finding the body of Paige Whitaker behind my bookstore. Since then, we've come across each other a few times. Unfortunately, there's usually a dead body involved. She had caused feelings to stir in me I hadn't felt since Autumn died. Gomez and I even went on a date, although it ended abruptly after finding a dead body. But that's a story for another day.

Gomez had asked me out to be her arm candy at a fancy fashion show at the Chapin Museum. I was aware she had a boyfriend, but she asked me to accompany her to the occasion because they had broken up. Now they are back together. Life moves on.

I asked Shelly the first question that came to mind with Gomez's voice in my head. "Has Brian's personality or demeanor changed recently?"

"We came here with a list of eight places to do reviews for. He had reached out to the owners to let them know we were coming. Often, we get free food out of the deal."

"Not a bad deal."

"It has its good and bad parts."

"What type of bad parts?

"Sometimes the food isn't very good."

"Oh. What do you do about your reviews if that's the case?"

She glanced at me. "We don't post them. We're not out to bring harm to any restaurant."

"That's a good thing. Keep the positivity."

"Exactly. But we did the first four fine. On the fifth one, Brian got into it with the owner."

"Got into it? Like a fight?"

"I'd say it was more of an argument, but they almost came to blows."

"Why?"

She crossed a shapely set of legs and tapped the knee that ended up on top. "This was a strange one. I didn't understand it at the time and still don't. I said we don't post reviews when we don't like the food. Brian gagged on camera when he bit into a hotdog. The owner was standing to the side, off camera, when it happened. When she asked what was wrong, he said the dog was disgusting. While I didn't care for the rough ambience of the place, I thought the food was terrific."

"Which place was this?"

Her face scrunched together in concentration. "I forget exactly. It was, like, a biker bar, but with pigs and wiener dogs."

"In Murrells Inlet?"

"I think that was the name of the town."

"Ah, you're talking about Big Hoggz Weiner Doggz."

"Yeah! That's it. It was a little," she paused and then gave the next word out of her mouth more weight, "*grungy* for my taste, but Brian wanted to go there."

"I know the restaurant. I've never been. Not my type of place, but they say the food's great."

"That was all I liked about the restaurant. On the greasy side, though."

"The grease comes with the area."

She smiled and attempted a laugh. "I've noticed."

"So, what happened with Brian and this owner?"

Her fingers drummed the end of one knee. "She didn't want us to run the video. I think Brian thought his reaction was funny after he got to thinking about it, and said he wanted to use it in a blooper reel. The owner was upset because you could see a neon sign with the name Big Hoggz Weiner Doggz in the background. He said that we would blur it out, then told me to grab the camera and head out to the van."

"He wanted you to leave while he confronted the owner?"

"Yes. He can get, um, heated when he's mad."

"Seems like a flimsy reason to fly off the handle. Who

escalated the argument first?"

"Brian, I think. It all happened so fast. Might have been the owner. I don't know. I was just appalled at the whole situation."

"You say the owner was a woman?"

"Yes, but she's one of those tough ones. Big. Tattoos all over. Shaved head. Wore leather. I was uneasy around her."

"Ah."

"If it would have come to blows, she would have sent Brian to the hospital." She eyed me up and down. "You look like you're in decent shape, but she could probably take you, too."

It was my turn to laugh. "Probably so. I've never thrown a punch in my life, nor do I plan to. Then what happened?"

"I went out to the RV, put everything in the back, sat in the van, and waited for Brian to come out. They burst out the door a few minutes later, shouting and cursing at each other."

"And they almost came to blows?"

"Almost. She had her fists clenched like she was ready to take a swing."

"Did he look like he wanted to strike her?"

Her head shook back and forth. "No. He just argued but retreated to the van and got in. They shouted at each other through the glass."

"What happened next?"

"The last thing she yelled was that if we posted it, she was going to come after him."

"Legally or physically?"

She crossed her arms. "I took it as physical. Like she'd beat him up. Or worse."

"What did he do with the video?"

"He wanted me to post it."

"Did you?"

Tears welled in her eyes again. "Yes."

CHAPTER
FOUR

Like a pop-up afternoon thunderstorm in Myrtle Beach, an ominous dark cloud settled over the conversation. My sense of foreboding grew stronger. I had a bad feeling about this, but I didn't want to reveal my suspicions to Shelly. The thoughts I had could be flat-out wrong. Sitting here in bumper-to-bumper stop-and-go traffic, there wasn't anything I could do about it except let it play out. I didn't want her to freak out further, if possible.

"Did you tell this to the police?"

A few seconds passed as Shelly thought about how to answer. Traffic moved slowly on this stretch of 501. This section of Conway consisted of numerous low buildings, gas stations, auto parts stores, and fast-food joints over rolling hills as we approached the Wright Boulevard intersection.

"No," she said after a minute. "I didn't think to do that when I was on the phone with them. Should I call them back?"

"It might not hurt to. Did you record them arguing in the parking lot?"

"No. I wasn't thinking. I was so flustered that I just sat there and cried."

"Can't blame you for that. Did you hear the owner threaten him?"

"I didn't. Brian told me she did. He laughed about it."

"He didn't take the threat seriously?"

She sat up straight in her seat and looked out the window. Her eyes went wide. She pointed ahead to our right.

"There he is!"

She pointed at a long, tall silver van with black trim along the bottom, a black pipe luggage rack on top, and a Mercedes logo on the front grill trying to get into our lane from a side street. Under the driver's side window was a magnetic sign with their reviewer's name, The 2 Foodie Nomads.

"Ooo. Nice wheels," I said.

"It's an Airstream camper van built on a Mercedes Sprinter chassis," she said as though she worked for Camping World.

I lived in an area of Surfside Beach next to the southernmost line of Myrtle Beach. The state park was seven minutes away if I hit the light to turn left on Business 17 from 544 just right. Between my house and the light were three humongous campgrounds, PirateLand, Lakewood, and the largest on the east coast, Ocean Lakes. RV dealerships surrounded all of them. Sometimes when traffic is backed up, I eye the smaller recreational vehicles, like the one Brian was driving, and dreamt about driving across the country. That was on my bucket list.

"I'm familiar with them," I said, knowing that a loaded one could cost a quarter million dollars.

She leaned forward and squinted. A truck in front of us in our lane stopped to let him out. Brian did so without so much as a courtesy wave. I glimpsed a man with a pale complexion before the turning motion of the camper van took him from view.

Shelly urged me to get moving, but I could only move so fast.

With an impatient tap on the steering wheel, I inched forward as a car pushed in from the same intersection Brian had come from. I hit the brakes. Shelly craned her neck, trying to glimpse the van, and pulled a phone from her pocketbook.

She tapped on the screen a few times and held it to her ear. "Come on. Come on. Pick up, Brian."

After a few seconds, she let out a cry of anguish and slammed the phone on her knee. "It keeps going straight to voicemail. I don't know why he doesn't answer."

"Maybe his phone is dead."

"That can't be. He kept it on a charger in the van all day."

"Hmm," I hummed.

"Hmm, what?" she demanded.

"It can only mean one of two things. Well, three if he lost the phone, but that's doubtful."

She turned to face me, but the traffic was moving again. My eyes were on the road, so I couldn't see her exact expression, but from her tone, it was likely between skepticism and annoyance. "What's the other two?"

"He either turned it off or he's avoiding your calls."

"Why would he do that?"

Instead of telling her my hunch, I said, "Why do you think he would do that? You know him a thousand times better than me."

Brian's RV was able to get into the passing lane, creating distance.

"Um, well. Hmm." She touched a hand to her chin. "He seemed downright giddy earlier talking about this surprise he has in store for us in Charleston on Tuesday. If it weren't for that, I would say he was trying to leave me." She laughed. It was cute. "But he wouldn't do that."

"Alrighty. Why isn't he answering your calls?"

"I don't know, to be honest. I've been trying to rack my brain for the last hour, trying to answer that question." Her voice hardened. "Try to catch up with him."

Checking the rear and side mirrors, I said, "I'll try if this traffic will let me."

For a moment, the lane to my left moved at a swifter pace. To my frustration, Brian was not merging back into the right lane. I flicked on my turn signal and waited. After two cars passed, the third let me in. I threw up a hand, thanking the driver who let me in as I pulled into the passing lane. For a few seconds, our lane moved faster. We crept up on Brian. Then another stoplight brought everyone to a halt.

There were now four vehicles between Brian's RV and the car next to us. Maybe twenty feet. Cars flowed across at the intersection.

Shelly placed a hand on the door latch and took in a deep breath.

"Are you going to try to catch up to him here?"

She breathed out. Her eyes flicked to the dozens of cars surrounding us. "I don't know. I'm scared."

At once, the cars crisscrossing at the intersection halted. The left turn lights glowed green in the middle lane.

"Better hurry if you are. Our light's about to turn green."

She took her hand off the door and clasped her hands together in her lap. "I better not. I won't make it in time."

"Don't worry. We'll catch up with him."

A junky, smoky truck idled in front of Brian at the light. When it turned green, the truck backfired and sputtered.

"Go, go," Shelly insisted.

The automobiles in my lane paid the truck no heed and sped by.

"You're almost there!" Shelly shouted.

A vein of excitement flowed through me. I felt like I was in a slow-speed car chase in a movie.

The sporty Nissan behind Brian lagged while the driver looked at his phone. I sped up and signaled into that lane.

"Yes! We're right behind him," Shelly said, clenching her fists and smiling. A tear emerged from the corner of her eye.

I gripped the steering wheel tighter. "I'll stay right behind him, and we'll see where he's going."

We followed him for a mile before we came to the Wright Street intersection. The light turned yellow. It did so at the point where you could either go faster to get through in time or come to an easy stop.

Brian floored it.

The cars in the right lane next to me stopped. I hesitated. Another light lay ahead. I saw it was turning red as well, and the brake lights came on the camper van. Out of the corner of my eye, I spotted a police cruiser sitting at the light in the crossing lane, waiting to go straight.

I glanced up at the light as it turned from yellow to red.

"Go!" Shelly shouted, but I didn't.

I slammed on the brakes. The Jeep's big tires screeched. The inertia rocked us forward in our seats. She smacked a hand on the dashboard.

We were first in line. A white mini-monster truck with its suspension tilted from the back to the front and chrome bumpers turned right off Wright and got behind Brian.

"Those trucks are so ugly," Shelly said. "The only place I've ever seen them is around here."

"Yeah. They call it the Carolina Squat. These kids raise up

the suspension in the front, add chrome, put on gigantic wheels, speakers, bright LED lights, you name it. I think they're trying to outlaw them in this state. Some weekends, they're all over the place."

"Where do they get their money to customize the trucks like that?"

"Beats me. Wealthy parents, I guess."

Brian's light turned green well before ours did. We were powerless as we watched the camper disappear around a bend.

I groaned. "I'm sorry."

She looked ahead but didn't see Brian. The Horry County police cruiser cruised past us on Wright. "That cop would have pulled you over and we would have lost him, then he might have really gotten away. It's okay. We'll catch up to him."

Her tone had made it clear that it wasn't, but I tried to assuage her anger. "I travel through here often. These lights either get you every time or you catch green on all of them. When this turns green, I'll floor it."

Her lips tightened in a smile, but she said nothing and kept her focus forward.

Our light turned green, and I pushed the Jeep as fast as humanly possible, which meant in this traffic, turtle speed. We hurried up and stopped at another red light. Ahead, we saw Brian's RV sitting at a different intersection fifty or so yards away. As the crossing traffic remained green, several vehicles pulled in behind Brian, including two tractor-trailers and the cop. They blocked Brian from view.

"Oh no," Shelly said. "I can't see him now. Again."

"He's there. We can catch up to him," I said with conviction.

Brian's light and our light turned green at the same time. I wanted to floor it, but the tractor-trailers took up both lanes and were in a race to see who could move the slowest. No one could pass them.

After a few miles, one passed the other and got into the slow lane. I weaved through traffic, trying to catch up to Brian. We traveled past Lake Busbee.

Brian and his campervan were nowhere in sight. Shelly released a cry of desperation. My jaw tightened with resolve.

Before long, we stopped at the intersection of 501 and 544. I pointed to our right. "I live down that way in Surfside Beach."

She nodded her head. "We did a video at a sandwich place called Dagwood's there on Tuesday."

"Popular place. Around the corner from my house."

"Which direction should we go?"

"You say you're staying at PirateLand?"

"Yeah."

"That's in that direction, too."

"Go there," she said. "Maybe that's where he was going."

"How much longer were your reservations for?"

"Two more nights."

"Okay." If Brian was as affluent as Shelly let on, then losing two nights' worth of camping fees would not hurt his bank account.

We wound past Coastal Carolina University and Brooks Stadium.

"I attended school here a long time ago," I said, trying to make casual conversation and take her mind off Brian.

"Oh. Nice."

I pointed at the stadium. "They just broke ground on it when I graduated."

"When was that?"

"The early 2000s."

"Oh. I was only a couple of years old then."

I laughed. "Thanks for my daily reminder that I'm getting old."

"Oh, sorry."

"No need to apologize. The older I get, the more I realize that age is relative. I don't feel my age. Sure, my knees and back creak more when I get out of bed in the morning." I pointed at the side of my skull. "It's all up here. I still feel mentally young, but with life experience. Like, you and Brian probably think you know everything."

She nodded but didn't speak.

"At least, I thought I did when I was your age," I said. "But, if thinking back on it, man, I was stupid. At least I had a wife to keep me grounded."

"What's her name?"

"Autumn." I left out the being dead part.

"What do you do now?"

"I own a bookstore on the Myrtle Beach Boardwalk and write books." I jerked a thumb at the cramped cargo hold in the back. "Just came from an author event in Marion."

"Oh, nice. What kind of books do you write?"

"Mysteries."

"Helping me find Brian is right up your alley."

"I don't know about that. I just create and solve complex puzzles on my computer screen and try to tell a good story along the way."

"I'm sure you do, but your mind must be trained to look at all the clues and try to sort everything out."

"Maybe."

She sat forward and craned her neck. "Ah man. I thought I saw him."

I had kept my eyes on the traffic going in both directions, in case he turned an about-face, but hadn't seen a sign of their camper. "Keep a lookout."

"I will." She settled in.

We saw no trace of Brian or the RV before reaching PirateLand.

CHAPTER
FIVE

When we arrived at the PirateLand entrance, they informed Shelly that they hadn't seen or heard from Brian. He hadn't been back since that morning.

We pulled out onto Kings Highway and headed for Surfside and Murrells Inlet. I knew where I wanted to go.

"I don't know what to do," Shelly said with her face buried in her hands.

The sun was on its final descent to the horizon. Splashes of orange and purple hung in the sky ahead. I put on sunglasses to shield my eyes from the glaring sun. She pulled down the sun visor.

She had no clothes or toiletries. Nothing except what was in her pocketbook.

"Can I make a suggestion?"

She looked up and turned her head to me. "Yes, please. Anything."

"Let's go to the hot dog place."

She raised a finger. "Anything except that."

"Hey, the owner's beef was with Brian. Not you."

"True. She was nice to me before that. Maybe he went there to smooth things over with her."

"Still doesn't explain why he left you."

"I still can't make any sense of it." She pointed out the window. "There's that Dagwood's."

"Yep. We just passed the turnoff to my house."

"Nice. You're kind of in the middle of everything."

"It is. We picked a nice spot to call home. Minutes from everything, even the ocean is a quick bike ride away."

"That's great. Can you smell the ocean at your place?"

"If the wind is blowing in the right direction, sometimes. I live just under a mile from the beach as the crow flies."

"After growing up on a farm, that sounds dreamy."

The idle chatter was a good way to keep her mind off the current predicament. She had sat back in her seat and relaxed somewhat. The ebbing of her tension helped me settle and think clearer.

"I grew up in Southern Ohio. We had the rivers and hills. I always wanted to live near the ocean. I remember the day I got the acceptance letter from Coastal just how happy I was. It didn't hit me how close I was going to be to the ocean until I moved into my dorm and me and my roommate drove down to the Pavilion that first night."

"That's a fun memory."

I grinned. "That's about all I remember from that night. There might have been a few beverages involved if you know what I mean."

The corner of her mouth curved up. "I do."

"What happened after you all left Big Hoggz? Was there any fallout from it? I take it you didn't see the owner again?"

Her eyebrows lowered. "No, but Brian acted differently after that."

The base of my neck tingled. "How so?"

She placed an elbow against the door and put a closed hand to her chin. "He was, I don't know, moodier. Maybe? Like, until then, he was fine. After that, he seemed to want to jaw and fight with the other three places we went."

"What were they?"

"Let's see. There was Fasta Rasta Pasta."

"Love that place. I could have Jamaican-Italian pasta with fresh seafood any day of the week."

"It's not a combination we've ever seen," she said. "And we've been all over the country just about. I enjoyed it."

"Did Brian act weird there?"

"He did. He went back and spoke with the owner, who's also the chef, while I was setting up the camera in the dining room. When Brian came back out, he said he was having second thoughts about filming. I asked him why, but he didn't answer. Sometimes he keeps stuff from me. I told him we could pack up and leave if he wasn't comfortable. But right then, the owner, Devon, came out with our food. It was too late to leave by then."

"What happened?"

"We ate and filmed. I loved it. He was ambivalent, but Brian loves him some pasta. It surprised me that he didn't care for it, although he put on a friendly face for the review and said good things, but I could tell."

"What about the owner?"

"He rocked back and forth on the balls of his feet and stood there with his arms crossed while watching us. It was a little unnerving, to be honest. I could tell he was ready for us to leave as soon as possible."

"Why didn't you?"

"Oh, we did, but we wanted to finish filming. The more content we put out, the more we earn from YouTube. It's work, and I didn't want the time to be wasted."

"What do you do with the money you collect from the videos?"

She snorted. "A lot of it goes to gas, but he lets me keep most of it. He closed his bank account and loaded the money in mine before we set off on this journey and uses it when he needs to. We'll withdraw cash now and then, but mostly the money stays put."

"Wouldn't it have been better if you had separate accounts for your travels?"

"Why do you say that? It's been fine so far." She recrossed her arms over her chest. Her tone was a tad bit defensive.

"What if you lost your bank cards? How would you get money then?"

"We'd have Brian's dad wire us some money," she said matter-of-factly.

"Well, okay then."

I wasn't her dad, nor was it my place to counsel her, but that seemed like a risky plan for traveling. When Autumn and I traveled, she would have cash hidden in several places along with a backup credit card in case I lost my wallet, or she lost her pocketbook. Wisdom comes with age. "I don't guess you have to buy much food doing what you do?"

She tilted her head to the side and smiled. "Nope. One of the perks."

"I bet. Where did you go after the Fasta Rasta Pasta?"

"Bombur's Bakehouse near Barefoot Landing."

"A place near and dear to my heart."

Bombur's was a smash hit from the minute its doors opened

last year. Bombur was the fat dwarf from The Hobbit. The restaurant was Hobbit, Lord of the Rings, and J.R.R. Tolkien themed. That was part of the draw. The other part was the cookies. Half-pound monstrosities loaded with toppings. People would wait in line for over an hour just to get inside.

I had been there several times and had met the owner. She seemed pleasant and hardworking.

"It was phenomenal. Reminds me of a place in Orlando named Gideon's."

"What happened there with Brian?"

"The filming and everything went fine. It was after that he said he wanted a couple of cookies to take with us back to the campground. I was packing up our stuff when he got into a shouting match with the cashier. He got upset that they wanted to charge us for the extra cookies."

"Did he think your recording there entitled him to unlimited cookies?"

"I guess so. That's one of the few things about him I don't care for. The sense of entitlement."

"He sounds like he came from a family where he got what he wanted."

"Not exactly. His dad was always hard on him. Sure, he had plenty of everything, but he and his dad would get into it."

"Get into it, how?"

"Brian tried to do his best, but it was never good enough for his dad. His dad would yell. Brian would yell back, defending himself. They'd go back and forth for days sometimes."

"And Brian was due to take over the business?"

"Yes. I think it was his dad's way of grooming Brian for the job."

"I can see that, even if the methodology is a little harsh."

"Don't get me wrong," Shelly said. "Brian loves his parents and all they've done for him. You sure ask a lot of questions, don't you?"

I held a hand to my chest. "I'm sorry. It's how I am. I'm a curious person and sometimes that gets me into situations I probably shouldn't be in."

She smiled. "Are you a cat?"

"Not the last time I checked."

"Just asking because I didn't know how many lives you had left if you are as curious as you say you are."

"After what I've been through, I have half of one left." I laughed. She asked a great question. Sometimes I bite off more than I can, or should, chew. "Back to Bombur's. What happened when he tried to get the free cookies?"

"The owner came out from the kitchen, grabbed Brian, and took him behind closed doors. He came out a few minutes later. His face was flushed. Said he didn't want to talk about it. So, we left."

"Post the video?"

"Of course. It turned out well. The interior of the place was amazing."

"It is. Made to look like the inside of Bilbo Baggins' home. Then where did you go?"

"Back to the campground."

"When was this?"

"Last night."

"Notice anything odd last night with Brian after getting back?"

"Not really," she said and paused. Her face softened into a gradual smile. "He was, uh, friskier than usual, though."

I kept my eyes forward and just nodded my head. I wasn't about to make eye contact after that comment.

"What about this morning? Where did you go? Had he gotten over whatever got him into a foul mood yesterday?"

"Yeah, he seemed to have moved on. I slept in. He got up early, stepped out, and took a long walk on the beach. He woke me up when he returned. He'd been waiting for this day since we arrived here."

"Why so?"

"We were going to go see one of his best friends from college."

"Who is that?"

"Dwayne Clayton."

"Why does that name sound familiar?"

"He owns the Grub N' Go breakfast place up on the Boardwalk."

"That's it!" I snapped my fingers. "I can walk there from my bookstore. I've met him. Autumn and I used to go there for breakfast all the time."

"Why don't you go anymore?"

I pursed my lips. "She passed away about three years ago."

She held a hand to her mouth. "I'm so sorry."

"No, it's okay. It happens."

"How did she die? She must have been so young."

"She was two years older than me." I hesitated. "She was a clerk at the courthouse and died of a heart attack at her desk one evening."

"That's horrible," Shelly said as she placed a hand on my arm. "I feel so bad for you. Do you have any kids?"

"We didn't." A burst of sadness bolted through me.

"That's so horrible. Are you okay now?"

"I am. Took me a few years, though." I lowered my chin. "Let's get back to Brian."

"Yeah, sorry to bring that up."

"Don't mention it. You didn't know. Tell me about Dwayne Clayton."

"He and Brian were best buds in college. Dwayne was another rich kid who received a large trust fund, like Brian, when they turned eighteen. A chunk of that went to fund their college education. Dwayne took what was left over in his trust fund, moved here, and opened the restaurant."

"It's been there for about five years, I think."

"Sounds about right. Brian has been out of college for about that long."

"Did everything go okay at Grub N' Go?"

"Not exactly."

"How so?"

"We ate our meal, did our review, then he and Brian went to Dwayne's office and closed the door."

"Were they yelling at each other?"

"Don't think so. Brian came out and was ready to go. His face was red. I don't think he said goodbye to his friend. I did."

"Did you find anything odd about the place?"

She stuck a finger to her lips. "The place? No. It was great. They make everything fresh there. Never frozen. A little cramped, maybe, but great."

"I sense a 'but' in there."

"Yeah, one thing was odd. I noticed this and mentioned it to Brian, but he didn't see the resemblance."

"What resemblance?"

"There were two people working there. A girl at the register and a guy on the stove. I thought they looked like us."

"How so?"

Shelly combed her hair with her fingers. "The girl was about my age and had blonde hair like me. The guy was like Brian, but maybe a little pudgier. Like I said, it was odd."

"Meh. The law of averages suggests that anything is possible like that. There are guys all over who look like me."

She snorted. "Sure. On the Hallmark Channel maybe."

My face turned red. "*Pfft*. Whatever," I said, brushing aside her compliment, "Then what?"

"We walked on the beach for a while until it was time to go to Conway."

"Did anything odd happen at The Trestle?"

"Nope. It was wonderful. Brian had the Pile Up Grilled Cheese. Goodness. He barely let me have a bite. What a flavor profile! I ordered the Salad Sampler Plate. I couldn't decide between one, so I ordered them all."

"Did he get into any fights with anyone there?"

"He didn't. He was his normal, courteous self again. We left there and went to the coffee shop near the trailer sales place where you picked me up after that."

"What happened at the coffee place?"

"We went in, ordered two lattes, and I excused myself to go to the restroom. He said he'd grab our coffees and be in the RV. When I came out, my latte was sitting on the counter. He and the camper were gone."

I didn't know what to say. To leave a sweet, innocent woman like Shelly, who seemed to have lived a sheltered life until they hit the road, all alone like that was beyond belief. Why would Brian do that?

"Well, hopefully he'll turn up, and you can get to your next stop."

"I sure hope so. I don't know what I'm going to do."

"I'll help you as much as I can. Like I said, I have some friends you might stay with tonight." I had a sudden flash of inspiration as we passed by the Inlet Square Mall in Murrells Inlet, headed for Big Hoggz Weiner Doggz on the MarshWalk. "I have a friend who I bet knows the owner up ahead. If she won't talk to us, I'm sure she'll talk to Chris."

CHAPTER
SIX

We veered left off Kings Highway toward the Murrells Inlet waterfront and MarshWalk. The area was famous for its collection of stellar restaurants on both sides of Outboard Lane. Throw in The Lazy Gator Gift Shop, ice cream booths, bars along the half-mile-long boardwalk, live music, spectacular views of a natural estuary, and even goats on their own island, the MarshWalk was a happening place.

The hot dog restaurant was across the street from the local favorite, Dead Dog Saloon, and next to The Lazy Gator. Thanks to one restaurant on one end of Outboard Lane, called Suck Bang Blow, this stretch of Murrells Inlet was an epicenter of the semi-annual Bike Week. Several restaurants dotted the landscape here that appealed to the Harley-Davidson riding crowd beyond the curiously named main biker joint.

Big Hoggz was one of them.

The restaurant looked like a squat building from the Old West with a full-length covered porch. They painted the wood slat siding green above the porch roof. The name of the restaurant was tacked on the siding with wood cutout letters painted taupe. Skeletons of three ancient motorcycles sat atop the porch roof. Vehicles and motorcycles with out-of-state license plates filled the parking lot.

A frenzy of people and cars danced in an unspoken rhythm as people either left or arrived. I drove past Big Hoggz and found a spot in an overflow parking lot as a tiny, old Hyundai backed out.

"We parked behind this place when we were here before," Shelly said as she unclipped her seat belt.

"What time of day did you come?"

"It was mid-afternoon Thursday, between the lunch and dinner crowds."

"Yeah, it's not too busy around here at that time," I said as I climbed out of the Jeep and walked around to Shelly's side.

We stood next to each other as we surveyed the scene. The sun was almost down. A half-moon loomed in the eastern sky. Venus shone brightly to its right. A faint tang of salty air clung to the air.

"Busier now," she observed. "What a pretty evening."

"It'll be like this until the wee hours of Sunday morning." I stood on my tiptoes and scanned the parking lots on both sides of the road. "I don't see Brian's camper anywhere."

"Bummer," she said.

"Let's go inside," I said, gesturing to the front entrance.

We wove around the parked cars to the front of Big Hoggz. Several people stood on the porch, listening for their names to be called for a table. One couple wearing leather had already treated themselves to the bar and were sipping on longneck bottles of Bud Light in one hand and half-smoked cigarettes in the other. A Journey song pounded through wireless speakers, vibrating the ground beneath our feet. This was not a place to come for casual conversation.

We skirted past them, trying to avoid the smoke, and walked

inside. Steve Perry singing about a wheel in the sky grew louder. Fitting for a biker bar.

Bodies filled every bar stool and table seat in the restaurant. People huddled over their smartphones on benches to either side of the front entrance, waiting for a spot. A host station stood inside the door. Two women, both wearing leather, tattoos, and short skirts conversed behind the podium. One used a grease pen on a laminated floor map indicating the tables inside to show the other hostess where to take the next party.

The main hostess looked up. Her hair was tied off in green pigtails. The style reminded me of something my friend Marilyn might wear. In a crackly voice, she called, "Nix! Party of six!"

To our left, two portly parents stood and collected three small children. The harried dad hefted a baby carrier and passed by in front of us. The infant's eyes bulged in response to the loud music. Mom followed. Her expression mirrored that of her husband. Two of the little kids wore headphones and couldn't be troubled to tear their eyes off their tablets. The oldest girl wore a huge smile across her face and a Guns N' Roses shirt.

"I guess we know who wanted to come here," I said into Shelly's ear. It was the only way she could hear me above the din.

She put a hand to her mouth to stifle a laugh.

We approached the hostess as the song changed from Journey to Motley Crue. She marked a table off on her table map as three people exited the restaurant, then looked up and said with a pronounced Southern drawl, "Can I help you? We have a thirty-five-minute wait. You could sit at the bar before that if any of those deadbeats leave."

I looked to Shelly to take the lead since she had been here. She held both hands on her elbows with crossed arms and rocked back and forth on the balls of her feet. Her eyes darted around the interior but didn't speak. She said Brian was the one who handled all the contacting of the restaurants. To me, she seemed like a shy country bumpkin out of her element.

It was up to me to take the initiative.

The hostess studied us. I wondered if she thought Shelly was my daughter or if I was a guy having a mid-life crisis trying to rob the cradle with a younger woman.

"Yes, we need to speak to Maddi."

The hostess leaned her elbows on the stand and popped a blue bubble of gum. "Not happening. She's busy."

"It wouldn't take long," I said. "We just need to ask her a few questions. It's about Shelly's fiancé, Brian."

The hostess tore her eyes off me and stared at Shelly. Then her eyes lit with recognition. "Wait, you're one of those food reviewers that was here the other day."

"I am," Shelly spoke up.

The hostess pursed her lips and shook her head from side to side. "That sure didn't go well."

"I know," Shelly said. "I agree. Brian acted like a butt when we were here, and I apologize for it. I was hoping to tell Maddi I was sorry before we leave the area."

The hostess looked at me, then back to Shelly. "I thought he said he wanted to ask the boss lady some questions."

"We do," Shelly said. "It's about Brian. I want to see if he came back and apologized or if she's seen him."

"I just came on duty a few minutes ago," the hostess said. "Haven't seen him."

"He disappeared on me," Shelly said and then turned away.

Her brow crinkled. "Disappeared? Whaddya mean

disappeared?"

"He left her behind at a coffee shop in Conway," I said.

"Whaddya mean he left you?" the hostess said, putting her hands on her broad hips.

I could tell we were going to keep going in circles with this woman until we either explained the situation or drew her a picture using her grease pencil. The pictures might work better, but my art skills weren't up to par for what we needed.

"That's just it," I said. "They stopped in Conway to get coffee. She went to the bathroom. When she came out, he was gone. Vanished. Vamoosed."

"Just like that?" the hostess said. Her neck was turning red. If Brian had been here, she might have popped him one.

"Yes, like that," Shelly said, placing three delicate fingers on the edge of the stand. "Look, I just want to learn what he said to Maddi. We're trying to figure out what he's up to."

"You and your dad here?"

Now it was time for my neck to flush.

Shelly laughed. "No, he's not my dad. He stopped to help me and brought me here."

"Oh," the hostess said. "Took him for your dad."

"Sorry to disappoint you," I said.

Then for the second time in as many minutes, the hostess's expression changed, and she pointed a finger at me. "Wait a dang minute. I've seen you before. You're that guy who goes around solving murders."

The redness spread from my neck to my face.

"Say what?" Shelly said, turning to me.

"Yeah," the hostess said. "He's become famous around here for helping the police solve a few murders."

"You said you were a curious person. You didn't tell me you solved crimes," Shelly said.

"I hadn't planned on it," I said.

The door opened as two couples got in line behind us. A server arrived at the hostess's side to see if he could help. She studied us for a beat, popped another bubble, and said, "Come on. I'll see if Maddi can talk to you."

"Thanks!" Shelly said.

The hostess held up a finger. "Just beware. On a night like this, Maddi is going to be super busy. She may or may not talk to you, and if she does, one, you're lucky, two, be quick about it."

"We will," I said, not knowing if we could hold up on our promise.

She led us around the periphery of the dining area to the back of the restaurant. The patrons gobbled down hot dogs loaded with toppings of all sorts, laughed, and had an all-around good time while shouting at the top of their lungs over the music. Multiple flat-screen televisions hanging from the walls showed a mixture of the Atlanta Braves baseball game and a Charlotte Hornets NBA Playoff game. The walls were decorated with Harley-Davidson, Indian Motorcycle, and Myrtle Beach Bike Rally pictures and signage. Next to the kitchen entrance, a black-and-white photo of the owner Maddi standing beside her chromed-out Harley at the Grand Canyon hung on the wall.

She stopped by the swinging door and said, "Wait here a sec. I'll see if she's available."

"Thanks," Shelly said.

A server opened the door with a tray of hot dogs. "Coming out!"

We stepped aside to let him pass. The hostess caught the door as it swung back and pushed it through so she could enter the kitchen.

Shelly and I stood against the wall, watching people eat.

My stomach gurgled. "It just occurred to me I never ran through Bojangles on our way through Conway."

"Oh, that's right. I'm sorry," Shelly said, slapping a palm on her forehead. "Brian and I had just eaten, so I'm still not in the least bit hungry. Maybe you could order something to-go here."

"Maybe. Let's see if we can talk to the owner first."

The server returned, edging past us. He shouted, "Coming in!" before entering the kitchen.

After he entered, the hostess and Maddi stepped out.

"Coming out!" Maddi bellowed.

"Here she is," the hostess said and retreated to her post.

Shelly's fear for Brian's safety at the hands of the woman before us was clear. Maddi towered over me. Her broad shoulders had caused her to have to shimmy to get out the door. Gray stubble covered her shaved head. Sweat dotted her heavy brow. Hard blue eyes bore into us. Her mouth was set in stone, as was her jaw. She wore a black apron with "The Boss Hogg" embroidered in silver script across the top.

My heart rate sped up. From the look on Maddi's face, she would not put up with anything that might waste her time. She flung a white dish towel over one shoulder after drying her hands on it.

"Shelly!" she said.

My eyes went wide as I resisted the urge to clear any wax out of my ears. Her voice was soft, like marshmallows covered with tiny rocks. If Disney ever needed someone to play an amusing but gruff female sidekick in a cartoon, Maddi was it.

"Hi Maddi. I need to ask you a question," Shelly said.

Maddi tilted her chin at me. "Who's this?"

"His name's Clark. He picked me up."

"Why did he pick you up? Brian not with you? I thought you two were attached at the hip?"

"We usually are," Shelly said.

Maddi cupped her chin. "That explains it."

"Explains what?" I said.

"Well, explains it a little," Maddi said.

Shelly stepped closer to Maddi. "Explains what?"

"Why you weren't here with Brian."

"Brian? When did you see him?"

Maddi looked at the wide leather watch on her wrist. "I reckon about half an hour or so ago."

CHAPTER
SEVEN

Shelly and I locked eyes. If we hadn't have stopped at the campground, we might have caught him.

"You mean he was just here?" I said.

"Come on," Maddi said, pushing open the kitchen door. "Let's go out back and talk."

After announcing that we were entering the kitchen, she led us past the expo line for the prepared dishes and into the kitchen. A line cook grilled hot dogs on a sizzling gas stovetop. Another guy worked the bubbling deep fryer basket. A lanky college-aged kid hustled putting baskets together with the toppings on the prepared hot dogs. It was all in a line, nice, neat, and organized. My slight OCD approved. A small stereo in the corner blasted rap music. A much different vibe to the music played out in the dining room.

We passed a thick silver freezer door before going through an exit at the rear of the building. The thumping music died away, and we stepped onto a sandy lot. I could hear the voices in my head again.

Maddi closed the door behind her and rubbed a hand across the stubble on top of her head. "That's better. Can't hear anything in there, but that's the way the customers like it. Second time I've been called out of the kitchen tonight. No one called out, so we're fully staffed back there. Kitchen can run on its own without me if that's the case."

"I'm glad we're not hurting your workflow," Shelly said.

"Don't worry about it," Maddi said in a sing-song voice. "Yeah, he came in here to apologize for his actions the other day and made sure there were no hard feelings. I wondered where you were."

"That was nice of him," I said. "Did anything seem off with him while he was here?"

"I could tell he was in a hurry. I mean, he was in and out of here right quick. He told me he'd had a bad coupla days and took it out on others. He was trying to make up for it."

"Shelly told me about your confrontation with him. What happened?"

"I was standing off to the side while they were filming their review. He bit into his BBQ Explosion Dog and gagged. That's our most popular dog. I made it myself to make sure it was perfect. We've never had that happen to anyone, and I wanted to make sure he was okay and didn't bite off more than he could chew."

"Then he got mad and started yelling," Shelly said. "I've never seen him like that before."

"Out of the blue?" I asked.

"Yup. I didn't know what to say," Shelly said.

Maddi closed her eyes and cocked her head to the side. "It was the darndest thing. Like he'd flipped a switch. He was cordial before that, but it was like he turned into a different person."

"I agree," Shelly said.

The hair on the back of my neck tingled. There was that feeling again. "Shelly said you threatened him."

Maddi rubbed her face. "Mmm-hmm. I shouldn't have done that, but he got me all hot under the collar. I have a bit of a temper and try hard to control it."

"Did you tell him not to post the video?" I asked.

Maddi shifted on the balls of her feet. "Yeah, that was the threat."

"You know they posted it, don't you?"

Maddi giggled. "I do."

"What's so funny?" I asked. "I would think a bad review like that might hurt business."

"Did you see how many people were here when you walked in?" Maddi laughed. "One bad review won't sink this place. Let's say someone watches this review and gets on Google to find the address. You know what they're going to see?"

"I don't," I answered.

"Over five-thousand five-star Google Reviews." She turned to Shelly. "It was the heat of the moment. He got in my face. I balled up my fists and almost punched the twerp but chose words over actions. I'm sorry."

"You shouldn't be the one to apologize," Shelly said. "It should be us."

"Not you, hun. You had nothing to do with it."

I caught a whiff of grilled hot dogs as a busboy opened the back door carrying a full trash bag. We stopped talking to let him pass and throw the garbage into a large green dumpster next to a fence.

After he went back inside, I said, "That was wise."

"Believe me, and no offense, Shelly, but I wanted to throttle that boy."

Shelly held up her hands. "None taken."

"Did he say where he was going?" I asked.

"He didn't, but he mentioned that he rubbed Devon at Fasta Rasta Pasta the wrong way too."

I turned to Shelly. "If Brian is going on a tour to atone for his unacceptable behavior, maybe he was talking about his next stop."

"Makes sense," Shelly said.

"I had the impression he might be headed there next," Maddi said.

"Okay then," Shelly said. "Thanks, Maddi! You've been a big help."

"Yeah, thanks." I gave an awkward thumbs-up.

"No problem." Maddi enveloped Shelly in a hug. The smaller woman almost disappeared into the restaurateur's embrace.

We peeled out from the MarshWalk a minute later, headed for Myrtle Beach and Fasta Rasta Pasta. I didn't go back in and get a hot dog, opting to go around the restaurant and back to the Jeep. Time was of the essence.

As I stopped on the street to let a family of pedestrians cross to Drunken Jack's, my stomach growled.

* * *

Shelly was quiet while she watched the people, the restaurants, and the inlet pass by to our right.

Silence made me uncomfortable. Made me want to talk to fill the air. The only way to get a person's thoughts is to get them to talk. I've learned the only way to make a person who's comfortable with quiet talk is to make them uncomfortable.

I said, "So, Brian left you high and dry in Conway to what?

Go on an apology tour? That doesn't make much sense."

Her face turned red as the Inlet Crab House fell into the rearview mirror. Instead of discussing the matter at hand (which I'd much rather do), she pounced on another subject. One that I don't like to discuss. "Excuse me. What's this about you solving murders? Are you a retired cop or something?"

"Nope. Just a mild-mannered bookstore owner who stumbled across the body of a friend last year."

"And you solved it? The murder?"

"I did."

"Uh-huh. But the hostess said you solve *murders*. Plural."

"Okay. I've solved four."

"Four? That's amazing. How did you do that? Why did you do that?"

As I merged onto Business 17 en route to Garden City, I had to think about how to answer. Her first question required time to detail if I wanted to. The second was one that hadn't been asked of me, but it was one that I've asked myself many times. Until now, I hadn't put it into words. "My wife and I were married for fourteen years before she passed. We met in college and got married shortly thereafter. I worked as a district trainer for Target for a long time, giving me a retail background. She worked her way up through the court system to become a court clerk. She had a love of books that my mom might only match."

Shelly smiled. "You know, they say a lot of guys marry a woman like their moms."

I laughed. "Yeah. I can see that. Here, the books were where their similarities ended. I've never met another who left me short of breath like Autumn did."

I couldn't help it, but at that moment, an image of Detective

Gina Gomez in the green dress she wore the night of the fashion show at the Chapin Art Museum a few months ago popped up in my mind. I stumbled, then continued, "Autumn had a heart condition, and we woke up every day knowing it could be her last. We opened our bookstore together, but she kept on working at the courthouse to help pay the bills. One morning, we woke up and took a walk on the beach at sunrise, grabbed breakfast at The Golden Egg in Surfside, gave each other a kiss, and went off to work. That was the last time I saw her alive."

"My heavens," she said, covering her mouth. "I don't know what to say to that. I'm so sorry."

I waved her off. "Don't worry about it. It's been three years."

"Goodness gracious. That's so sad."

Instead of dwelling on the factory of sadness that was the aftermath of Autumn's death, I cut to the chase. "After that, I threw myself into my business and then helped my parents settle into their new house here. Anything to keep my mind off not having her with me. I was numb for a long time, trying to move on as she would have wanted me to do. It was so hard." I paused, thinking about those dark moments that involved way too much bourbon. "I was like Bill Murray in Groundhog Day, doing the same thing over and over each day with no purpose in life. Stuck in a rut. Big time. Then one morning, I came across the body of my friend Paige Whitaker behind my bookstore, and something possessed me to figure out who did it."

We pulled up to a stoplight in front of the Kroger grocery store in Garden City. I looked over at Shelly. Her mouth hung open. "Holy cow. That's the saddest and craziest story I've ever heard. So, you didn't stop at solving one murder. You solved three more."

"Those just kinda happened. They've found a way to appear since I found Paige."

"Why don't you leave it to the cops?"

"I generally do. They tell me to stay out of it, for the most part. I remember seeing Paige's husband looking so lost and dejected after her death. It hit me that he was me the night I learned of Autumn's death. I had no clue what to do. It made me want to help him and others, if possible, without stepping on the police department's toes."

"Is that why you stopped to pick me up?"

"Yeah. When I saw you screaming into your phone and then hang up, you had that same look. I had to help."

"Thank you," she said. "I might still be standing in that mobile home lot if it weren't for you."

"Don't mention it. At least now we have a trail to follow with Brian."

"We do." Her voice hardened. "I'm going to skin him alive when I find him."

I couldn't blame her for feeling that way. I drove on, hoping that someone else didn't have a reason to skin him alive, too.

CHAPTER
EIGHT

Fasta Rasta Pasta sits at the end of a strip mall sandwiched between 13th and 17th Avenue South in Myrtle Beach. Badcock Furniture, Big Lots, and Food Lion are the anchor stores in the shopping plaza. A Jamaican flag precedes the glowing neon letters of Fasta Rasta Pasta above a covered walkway.

The two rows of parking on this end of the lot were almost filled. Word was getting out about this Jamaican-Italian fusion restaurant, and tourists and locals alike flocked to it.

I found a spot at the far end and parked. I didn't see their camper van in the lot. My stomach rumbled.

"Quick question," I said.

Shelly gripped the handle of the door, eager to see if Brian was inside. "What is it?"

"On this food tour of yours, has Brian changed? Like, with his appearance?"

She cocked her head to the side. "Yeah. He has. He's grown out a beard and put on a few pounds." She laughed and patted a trim belly. "Of course, with all the food we've had, it's hard not to pack on the pounds."

I ate out a lot after Autumn's death and put on some unneeded weight. It was only within the last year that I started being more conscientious about what I ate and exercised more. With all that had happened since I discovered Paige Whitaker's body, I'd dropped about fifteen pounds. Yay me.

"I can understand," I said.

"Why do you ask?"

"Just trying to get inside his mind."

"Oh, okay."

Thankful that she didn't ask a follow-up question, I opened the door. The aromas of spiced chicken, beef, and fish greeted us as we exited the jeep. The beat of reggae music thumped through speakers emanating from the restaurant.

Like Big Hoggz, people waited for tables outside the door. Like Big Hoggz, we were able to speak to the owner of Fasta Rasta Pasta, Devon Gordon.

Within a few minutes of entering, we stood out back with the gangly restaurant owner. Long dreadlocks bounced around his head as he bobbed up and down. Devon was a bundle of wiry energy. He wore a tie-dyed shirt with the restaurant's name on the chest and black jeans. His head was topped with a knit red, green, yellow, and black Rasta beanie.

A row of pine trees edged the back lot of the strip mall. The pavement was wide enough for delivery and garbage trucks to squeeze by. A big green dumpster stood outside the door. Several empty bottles of Caribbean rum lay at its base.

"Ya boy was jus' here," he said as I closed the back door behind me and stepped out into the night air, which carried a faint skunky odor.

"Brian was here?" Shelly asked.

"Ya mon," Devon replied. "He wanted te say his apologies. We hugged it out, and he got going fast."

I asked, "Did he say why he came back to apologize?"

Devon looked from me to Shelly and bounced on the balls of his feet. "Dis your dad?"

My face got hot. Shelly laughed.

"No," she said. "Brian abandoned me in Conway. This is Clark. He picked me up and offered to help find him."

Devon scratched the top of his beanie hat. Dreadlocks swayed. "Dat's bad, mon. No good. Why would he do dat?"

"That's what we're trying to figure out," I said. "What happened here that made him need to come back?"

Devon wiped away the sweat from his brow. "Che. Here's the ding, mon. Brian might've caught my two cooks doing something out here dey weren't supposed to be doing."

"He said nothing to me about it," Shelly said.

I looked from Shelly to Devon. "What were they doing?"

The tall man cocked his head to the side, pointed at the bottles at the base of the dumpster, pinched a thumb and forefinger to his lips, and did a sharp intake of air.

That explained the skunky scent. "I see."

Devon explained, "I was showing him te operation while Shelly set up her camera out front when Brian and I came out back here."

"And your workers were doing some, uh, recreational activities?" I asked.

"Che."

"What happened next?"

"Ya boy's face got all red. I could practically see te steam comin' out his ears." Devon shook his head from side to side. His dreadlocks swayed in sync. "He didn't say another word and went back inside and out to the dining room."

I turned to Shelly. "Do you remember this? How did Brian seem to you after he came out of the kitchen?"

"He wasn't back there long," she answered. "I was still setting up the camera on the tabletop tripod and getting the recording software going when he returned. He said little until I started rolling the camera."

"What happened with the two cooks?" I asked Devon.

He bit the corner of his lips and made a sound. "I sent dem boys home. Dey were stoned."

"Has this happened before?"

The man looked at the sky before answering. "No, mon. Never. First time. Last time, too."

That was a lie. I pointed at the empty liquor bottles on the ground. "Did you not at least have them clean up after themselves?"

"Oh, I guess not," Devon said. "Garbage pickup isn't for another two days. It would have gotten cleaned up den."

"What if the food sanitation people popped in for an inspection?"

Shelly stayed quiet during the conversation. She seemed content to let me handle the questioning. I wondered if she took a backseat when speaking to restaurant owners when Brian was around. Was she shy or just scared of what was happening to her?

His dreads swayed while he rocked his head. "Dunno, mon. We'd be busted, I guess."

"What happened to the workers?"

"I popped them good and told dem not te let it happen again."

"Are they here tonight?"

"One is. You passed him on our way through the kitchen."

He must have been talking about the gawky, pale,

college-aged kid with bleach blond hair. "What about the other?"

"His girlfriend is graduating from te technical school this weekend, so I let him off dis weekend to celebrate."

Given what we already knew about the two cooks, I had a good idea of what their graduation celebrations entailed. "What happened after you sent the cooks home?"

Devon splayed a large hand over his chest. "I did the cookin'. You want something done right, you do it yourself, right mon?"

"Not if it's brain surgery," I said, but I got his point. "You wanted to present the best dish possible, especially knowing what Brian saw out here."

"Dat's right. I cooked up the bess two plates of food I have ever cooked before."

Shelly chimed in. "I thought they were stupendous."

Devon bowed his head. "Thenk yuh."

"What did you have?" I asked.

"We had the Rasta Pasta and Reggae Lasagna," Shelly said, looking to Devon for confirmation.

"Dat's right," he said.

"What's in those?" My stomach was hurting so much that I hoped the description of food would help satisfy my hunger. I was wrong.

Devon's description made it worse. "Ah, yeh. The lasagna is like regular lasagna, but with steamed callaloo and spicy tomato sauce."

"And it was spicy," Shelly said, "but so decadent."

"Sounds good," I said. "What about the other dish?"

"It was dope," Shelly said. "It made me see why people love this place."

"Te Rasta Pasta is our specialty," Devon said with a touch of pride. "Fluffy, house made gnocchi sauteed in alfredo sauce served with ackee and saltfish. Jamaica's national dish."

"Sounds divine," I said.

"It was," Shelly said. "Which made Brian's reaction more puzzling."

"How so?" I asked.

Shelly crossed her arms. A car horn honked in the distance. "Like I mentioned, Brian loves Italian and Jamaican food by themselves. This place mixes the best of both worlds. It completely baffled me as to why he didn't like it."

"Could it be," I said, "that after his experience out here that he didn't want to give this place the publicity you would have given? That by saying he didn't like the food, whether he did or not, that got you out of doing the video, but still got you free food?"

"I hadn't thought of it like that," Shelly said.

"Could be, mon," Devon said.

"Maybe he did enjoy the food but faked his disgust to get out of shooting the video."

"Makes sense. I thought it was so weird that he didn't like the food." She turned to Devon. "I've had nothing like this in all our travels. It was phenomenal."

"Thenk yuh," Devon said again. His pride showed in his work. That much was apparent. It seemed like he took Brian's critique to heart but understood that Brian finding the two men getting stoned while on the clock tarnished whatever opinion he was going to have of the dishes.

"So, Brian came and apologized?" I asked.

"Che."

"It sounds like you should have been the one apologizing to

him," I said.

"Innit bruv," Devon agreed. "I did several times. Even sent him messages, which he never returned. I'm jus thankful that he didn't run the video."

"What did he say?" I asked.

"Jus, no hard feelings. He said his stomach hadn't been well and maybe the spiciness of the dishes rubbed him the wrong way. He said if dey had the time, that dey would have come back and done us proppa."

"That it?" I said.

"Dat's all, mon," Devon said. "Den he skipped out here."

"Did he say where he was going?" Shelly asked.

"Don't recall what it was called," Devon said. "Something wit cookies and dwarves, I dink."

Shelly and I locked eyes and said at the same time, "Bombur's Bakehouse."

"Yee, dat was the spot," Devon said.

We thanked Devon for his time.

"Walk good," he said, and we rushed back to the Jeep.

I almost grabbed a roll off a plate on our way back through the kitchen, but from the urgency with which Shelly darted through the doors on her way out to the Jeep, I didn't take the time to do it. Besides, I'm not a thief.

My stomach roiled as we sped out onto King's Highway, headed for North Myrtle Beach and an almost magical bakery, passing a hundred restaurants along the way.

CHAPTER
NINE

As we approached the Myrtle Beach Boardwalk and 4th Avenue N, I pointed out the window on her side. "My bookstore is down that street."

Shelly looked up from her lap and in the direction I indicated. "Oh, that's nice," she said without a trace of enthusiasm. "What is he up to? I could kill him."

"Whoa, whoa. Don't say that," I said. "You never know what will happen. There might be an innocent explanation for all of this."

She crossed her arms. "Oh, yeah. Like what?"

That's what I get for opening my mouth and speaking without considering what I'm about to say, especially since I didn't think there was an innocent explanation behind Brian's actions. "Uh. Um. Maybe he's looking for that perfect gift to give you before departing Myrtle Beach."

She blew a burst of air through her lips. "Yeah, whatever. Not Brian. I mean, he's great and all, but never been the gift-giving type. Try again."

"There's a first time for everything."

"Not this time."

"Has he done this kind of thing before? Leave you stranded?"

"No."

"See. This is the first time for that."

She squeezed her arms tighter together and shrunk down in her seat. That wasn't the most helpful thing I could have said. She was looking to me for guidance and support, which I'm always happy to give. She's the stereotypical damsel in distress, and I'm the brave knight that has come to her rescue. Except I'm not looking to wed her. That would be like marrying my daughter. Almost.

"Look," I said. "We'll find him. We've followed his trail this far. Someone is going to have an answer, or we're going to stumble upon him at one of these stops. If he's headed to Grub N' Go, at this time of night, he might have to stand in line for an hour, especially as busy as the Grand Strand is tonight."

Her shoulders deflated. "I guess you're right."

I flicked off the points with the fingers on one hand. I wrapped the other around the steering wheel. "He almost picks a fight with the woman from Big Hoggz. Gags on the food from Fasta Rasta Pasta. Gets into an argument with the people at Bombur's Bakehouse. Same with his buddy Dwayne Clayton at Grub N' Go this morning. Then you go to The Trestle in Conway and that goes fine. Right?"

Shelly ran the events through her head. "Yes, sounds about right."

"And he had displayed no type of anger directed at any food establishment before."

"No. Never. He'd bend over backward to help some restaurants."

"How so?"

"Let's say we pick a spot we want to go. I contact the owners or managers and set it up. We do research before going. That way, we know what to expect. With Brian's background in helping the family business and his education, he knows how good restaurants are supposed to run. Sometimes he'll find that, for example, a place has great food and glowing reviews, but when we get there, we find that the business is struggling, and the owner doesn't know why. Brian will talk to the owners about it, and sometimes he'll have us stick around for a day or two while he digs in and tries to help them right the ship."

"Sounds like what my buddy Chris used to do before moving here. Go on."

"He'll give suggestions on how to improve workflow and cash flow, and then we'll go on our merry way. He never asks for consulting fees, nor does he mention it in any of our videos. If we're at a place where the food is great, but they're suffering on the business side, he'll make sure they're on the right track before we leave town."

"Sounds like a nice guy."

Shelly smiled and looked out the window. "He is."

Having her in a better frame of mind, I said, "Circling back to his recent actions, which you say aren't the norm."

"Correct."

"Why now? What triggered him to act that way and then disappear? Anything happen at the restaurant you went to before Big Hoggz?"

"Hmm," she traced a finger over the door latch.

I feared for a moment she was going to open the door and roll out stuntman style, but she didn't—to my relief.

"That would have been 1229 Shine," she said.

"In Market Common?"

"I think that was the name of the area. Cool place."

"Yes, it is. I love the folks at the Barnes and Noble there."

"Even though you're competitors selling books?"

"Not strictly speaking," I said. "They're a national, well-known brand. When you walk into one, you know what to expect. My bookstore, I guess, is similar, but on a much smaller scale, and most of my business relies on tourism. Locals don't go to downtown Myrtle Beach that much during the travel season. Market Common is far enough away from the action that many locals are comfortable not having to worry about being surrounded by tourists who don't know where they're going. My wife used to get her hair done at the Dolce Lusso Salon down the street from B&N. 1229 Shine is a great place to hang out."

"Great food, too. Anyway, all went well there. Their grouper bites are next level."

"I agree." My stomach did a backflip as I recalled the last time I had that bowl of deliciousness.

"What about between you two? Any fights or disagreements?"

"Nope," she said. "We'd been fine. We're getting close to wrapping up our adventure together before he joins the family business."

"Interesting," I said as we passed the Tanger Outlets to our right.

Darkness tried to overtake the evening, but the neon lights of Myrtle Beach pushed back, as they do every night. An endless stream of restaurants, t-shirt shops, banks, grocery stores, and gas stations whooshed by as we made our way toward North Myrtle Beach and Barefoot Landing. I rarely get up this way, but when I do, it's as I pass through on my way to Wilmington.

I always think of North Myrtle as more touristy, and I'm around that enough at the bookstore.

When I'm not heading into North Carolina, Barefoot Landing often is the destination, particularly for the Crooked Hammock Brewery. The Landing has two popular music venues, for the occasions when I take in a concert—the Alabama Theatre and House of Blues—with multiple dining establishments—because of course, we're in Myrtle Beach—and an eclectic mix of shopping.

After driving by Arcadian Shores and Briarcliffe Acres, we passed a sign welcoming us to North Myrtle Beach, the home of Vanna White. Before long, we reached Barefoot Landing. The large shopping complex had multiple entrances at stoplights. LED signs along the highway advertised concerts at the Alabama Theatre and House of Blues. Another bright sign past the second entrance displayed pictures of wine slushies at Duplin Winery. Jimmy Buffett's sister owned a restaurant at the back of Barefoot named Lulu's. The famous golfer, Greg Norman, had an Australian steakhouse near that part of Barefoot.

"I didn't know Vanna White was from here," Shelly said.

"Yeah, she's the darling of North Myrtle Beach," I said. "Want to hear my idea for a themed restaurant?"

"Yeah, sure."

"With famous people putting their names on restaurants in North Myrtle Beach, Vanna needs a restaurant called 'Wheel of Food Fortune.' Diners would go in, spin three Wheel of Fortune style wheels. Separate ones for the appetizer, entrée, and dessert. Whatever the wheel landed on, that was your meal. What do you think, Ms. Restaurant Food Blogger?"

She laughed. "I don't know how that would go over with

picky eaters, but I'd be all for it."

"Maybe they can have two chances at the wheel," I said.

"That's not a bad idea," she said.

"But you don't think it's a good idea?"

"I mean, it has merit. With her being from here, it would bring a crowd."

I entered Barefoot at the entrance that went between Dick's and Wild Wing Cafe before getting to the open parking lots in front of the Alabama Theatre and Flying Fish Market. Bombur's Bakehouse occupied a spot on a strip in front of the Intracoastal Waterway beside River City Cafe.

I parked, got out of the Jeep, and immediately regretted it. A mélange of seafood and hamburger aromas hit me like a Mack truck. Holding a hand over my stomach was all that kept me from doubling over.

"Are you okay?" Shelly said, joining me in the lot.

"I'm just starving is all," I said.

She reached out a hand and patted me on the right shoulder blade. "Oh, you poor thing. Here I've been having you whisk me all over going to these restaurants. I'm so sorry. You haven't eaten, I forgot."

I waved her off. "No, it's okay. You need to stay hot on Brian's trail."

"Look, I know this bakery isn't a dinner place, but let me at least buy you a cookie here."

Ordinarily, a cookie wouldn't put a dent in the hunger that I had. However, these half-pound monstrosities at Bombur's Bakehouse might do the trick. I just wouldn't tell my mom that I had a cookie for dinner. At this time of night, the line might not be too long.

She looked around the parking lot. "Don't see our RV here."

"This is a big place. He could have parked in several areas and walked over here."

"Hopefully."

As we approached Bombur's Bakehouse, as always, I couldn't help but smile. It looked like a whimsical American version of Bag End, Bilbo Baggins's legendary Hobbit home from *The Lord of the Rings*. On film, the house had a curved roof covered with grass. Bombur's Bakehouse here in Barefoot Landing had a flat roof but was covered with fake grass. Tall bushes flanked either side of the front door and ivy climbed from the ground to the roof, obscuring sections of the cream-colored exterior. Fragrant flower shrubs lined the front of the Bakehouse in places where there weren't bushes.

Despite having to conform to modern building design, the Hobbit home's most notable feature was present. A round wooden door painted a bright green stood open between two rounded stained-glass windows where hungry shoppers could enter. Even if you had never heard of J. R. R. Tolkien or *The Hobbit* and *Lord of the Rings*, Bombur's Bakehouse would still stand out. The interior of the house matched the attention to detail on the outside. River City Cafe sat to its left. That's where the amazing hamburger smell emanated from. A sitting area lay to the side in between Bombur's and Flying Fish on the other side, filled with wooden benches and surrounded by a thick hedge. The seats were filled with happy cookie eaters.

Normally, Bombur's Bakehouse had a line stretching down the sidewalk, almost to Taco Mundo. Right now, only three people waited outside the door. The parking lot had emptied out. The Bakehouse wouldn't be open for much longer.

"I think we came at the right time," I said to Shelly as we got to the back of the line.

"You're right," she said. "When Brian and I were here before, people had to wait almost an hour to get inside."

"It's worth it once you do."

She craned her neck and tried to see who was behind the counter. "Don't see the owner Izzy, but I think the assistant manager is up there."

The architecture of Bombur's Bakehouse wasn't the only thing that brought in people. It was what they baked inside. Half-pound cookies of several varieties, which changed monthly. Each was unique. They made some cookies to fit certain characters or locations from Middle Earth, the world Tolkien created. Others held familiar flavors. The straight Mt. Doom Chocolate Chip Cookie did the trick for me.

A few minutes later, we stood before a short woman wearing a frumpy frock, pointy ears, and a name badge that identified her as Jessica. She recognized Shelly.

"Why aren't you with your man?" Jessica said from behind the counter.

A glass case in front of Jessica displayed the varieties of cookies remaining. There weren't many. I spotted a White Chocolate Gandalf's Beard cookie with my name all over it. Beside it was a pistachio-covered Gollum's "My Precious" Cookie.

Shelly crossed her arms. "We got separated."

"How did you do that? I thought you two were inseparable?"

"I thought so, too," Shelly said. "But it happened. Have you seen him?"

"Yeah," Jessica said. "He left here about ten minutes ago."

Shelly turned to me and gave an exasperated sigh. "Just missed him."

I asked the woman, "Did he say why he was here?"

"Yeah. For a couple cookies and to see if Izzy was in." Jessica nodded. "Izzy doesn't work on the weekends. I run the place when she's not here. She's at home with her kids at this time of night."

"Did you tell Brian where she lived?" I asked.

"No, but I sent her a message saying that he needed to speak with her. Something about what happened here the other day."

I had already gotten part of the story from Shelly, but I needed to know more. "I wasn't here," I said. "What happened?"

"I was in the back when it started." She turned to Shelly. "I watched you two do your video, then went back to work. It all seemed to be fine to me, but then I'm back in the kitchen and I hear Brian shouting at Carla. She was the cashier on duty that afternoon. Izzy was back there with me. We both came out, and Izzy asked what was wrong. Brian was screaming something about free cookies and that your video was going to make our business boom."

"Which it already was," I added.

"Exactly," the woman said. "It's good exposure, but it's not like we were going to go out of business tomorrow without their review."

"I had packed up our stuff," Shelly said, "when Brian went off. During his rant, I left out of embarrassment. After you and Izzy entered the picture, I didn't see what happened."

"It wasn't much," Jessica said. "Izzy straight up threw him out and threatened to call the police if he returned."

"When you saw Brian come in tonight, were you under

instructions to call the cops?"

Jessica curled her lip. "Nope. I took what Izzy threatened as more of a bluff. She's a tough woman."

"Like Maddi down at the hot dog place," Shelly said. "Izzy could probably take Brian in a fight."

This conversation was going nowhere. The clock was ticking, and Brian was getting farther and farther away. I said, "Look, Jessica. Brian left Shelly stranded alongside the road this afternoon in Conway."

Jessica gasped, holding a hand up to her mouth. "Oh, you poor dear. Why did he do that?"

"That's what I'm trying to figure out," Shelly said. "We've been to two other places where he might have gone."

"We picked up his trail in Murrells Inlet and followed it to here," I said.

"You must be an excellent tracker," Jessica said.

I tilted my head to the side. "I have good instincts."

Jessica's eyes narrowed. "Now that you mention it, you look familiar."

I didn't want to get into why I might look familiar to her and brushed her comment aside. "Many people look like me."

Jessica looked me up and down. "Yeah, in Hollywood maybe."

My cheeks warmed. "Thanks."

Jessica pulled out a notepad from under the cash register and scribbled something on the top sheet. She ripped it off and handed it to Shelly. "I'll get in trouble for doing this, but here's Izzy's cell number. Call her or send her a message explaining what is going on. I'm sure she'll help. She has a soft spot for women who have been wronged by a man."

"Is she that way from personal experience?" I asked.

"Yes," Jessica said, "but that is not for me to discuss."

"Did he indicate where he might go next?"

To our shared disappointment, Jessica said, "He didn't."

"Bummer," Shelly said.

Jessica put a finger to her chin. "You know, we did talk about the *Lord of the Rings* for a few minutes."

"That's odd," I said. "If he has a plan here, why would he stick around to talk about that?"

"Oh, he loved the movies," Shelly said. "I remember when he used to dress up as Samwise Gamgee at Halloween parties."

Sam was Frodo Baggins's childhood friend in the books and accompanied the young Hobbit on his quest to cast the one Ring into the fires of Mount Doom. After seeing the picture of Brian that Shelly showed me, I could see the similarity.

"Was there anything about the films that you discussed specifically?"

"Yeah," Jessica said. "It was weird."

"What was weird?" Shelly asked.

"You know at the end of the first movie, *The Fellowship of the Ring*, after the fight where Boromir gets killed and Frodo feels guilty and tries to strike out on his own?"

"Yeah, he's getting into a raft to cross the river when Sam comes running after him," I said.

"Right," Jessica said. "Brian asked me what I thought would have happened had Frodo made his escape without Sam."

A shiver rolled up my back. Frodo and Sam were the closest of friends on an epic journey in The Lord of the Rings, similar to what Brian and Shelly were doing, minus danger lurking around every turn. At one point, Frodo tried to go off on his own to protect Sam from peril. Was Brian trying to protect Shelly from something?

That wasn't good. We had to run. Like Brian was doing.

CHAPTER
TEN

Shelly followed up on her promise of buying me a cookie. In fact, she paid for two. The White Chocolate Gandalf's Beard and Mt. Doom Chocolate Chip Cookie. I was going to get a sugar high off them, but I had felt light-headed as we returned to the Jeep. Right now, any food was welcome. If I would have seen a partially eaten cookie on top of the trash can inside, I would have grabbed it.

After we shut the Jeep's doors and clicked our seatbelts into place, I opened a thin cardboard box, in the shape of a treasure chest that contained the two cookies. I lunged at Gandalf's Beard first and almost devoured the half-pound cookie in two bites. Never had anything tasted so fulfilling and filling at the same time.

With my mouth half-full of cookie, I said, "Grub N' Go Eats should still be open. That was the only place we haven't been where Brian caused a scene, right?"

"Yup. That's it," she said, then asked, "What do you think Brian was getting at, talking about Frodo trying to run?"

Here it was. The feeling that I'd had since Shelly told me her story. I hadn't wanted to say it, but I saw no way around it. I softened the blow by first saying, "Now, this is just a hunch. Doesn't mean it's true or will come true. You're a beautiful, smart young woman, and I don't know why he would do this, but I think…"

Shelly had me fixed with an intense stare. She hung on to every word. "You think what?"

"I think he's leaving you."

Instead of displaying shock, she sat back in her seat and nodded her chin up and down. "That's what I was afraid of."

"But that opens up several questions."

"Like what?"

I swallowed the bite and took another. We still sat in the parking space. Tired shoppers coursed through the parking lot, trying to find their vehicles under the streetlights.

"Like, he has to know that if he goes back home, you'll find him, and he'll have to confront this very horrible thing he's done to you." I didn't mention the flip side of that thought. I needed her to make that connection.

She did.

Her eyes widened. "You mean, he's not going home?"

"Maybe. Seems like it to me." I took another bite of cookie and said between chews, "You embark on this year-long journey before he's due to take over running his father's business. You say his dad is hard on him. My thought is, what if Brian doesn't want to run the business, but couldn't tell his dad? He waited until it was almost time to return home to disappear."

Shelly nodded. "I'm following you so far. That makes sense. He wasn't in love with what he was going to do once we returned to Louisiana. What about me, though? He loved me. At least, I thought he did. He was the one who brought up getting married next spring. Not me."

"And you said that you'd talked about kids too, right?"

"We had. Even had names picked out for the first born depending on if it was going to be a boy or girl."

I tapped the steering wheel as the neon lights of Myrtle Beach flowed past. "You said there had been no fights between you two or anything, so it's not like he was leaving you out of anger or hate."

She shrugged. "I know."

"Well, let's head to Grub N' Go. See if he's been there."

"Hopefully, his friend Dwayne will be there. He might know more than the others."

"Let's hope so. Can you send Izzy a message or call her?"

"I'll send her a message right now."

While she set about doing that, I pulled up behind a truck at the stoplight leading out of Barefoot Landing. I got us back out on Kings Highway and headed back south to the Boardwalk.

"Done," she said, and started to put her phone away, but didn't. "I'm going to try Brian again."

"Do it," I said. It seemed like a fruitless endeavor. One that would end in the same disappointment that she'd had all afternoon, but whatever comforted her.

She dialed and held the phone up to her ear. The radio in the Jeep was off. A faint ringing sound came from her phone. She turned to look at me with wide eyes. "It's ringing!"

"That's a first."

A second later, her encouraged disposition deflated. She took the phone from her ear and stared at the screen. "Never mind. Now it went to voicemail."

"But it rang once?"

"Yes."

"I'm no genius with cell phones," I said, "but that sounds

like you dialed when he had his turned on. Try him again. See what it does."

She did. This time, the call went straight to voicemail. "Must've turned his phone off. I wonder why he would turn it on if he didn't want me to call him."

"Maybe he needed to call someone."

"But who?"

"Beats me. You'd be the one to know who."

She squirmed in her seat. My statement appeared to make her uncomfortable. Why? Then she turned the tables and made me uncomfortable, although I couldn't realize a reason for her to do so. To this point, I had asked her a lot of questions about the world in which she and Brian existed but had revealed little about myself.

Perhaps to divert my attention or she was genuinely interested, she said, "Tell me about your wife."

CHAPTER
ELEVEN

A lump formed in my throat. When I'd spoken about her in the past year to anyone, it was mostly about the circumstances of her death. She had died of a heart attack at her desk one evening while working late at the City Courthouse in Myrtle Beach. We both had known any day could've been her last, as doctors had diagnosed her with a heart problem at a young age. All it would've taken was for one beat to go awry and that would be it.

That is what it appeared to be that evening, until Detective Gomez confided in me that she thought that Autumn had been murdered all along. She had been on the scene with the lead detective, Ed Banner, to investigate Autumn's death. Gomez said that Banner had barely given Autumn a look before declaring that there would be no need to investigate. The coroner had backed that up by confirming a death by a heart attack. Not knowing Gomez's suspicions yet, I had chosen not to have an autopsy performed. She had been cremated. I'd chartered a ship to go three miles out into the ocean and International Waters to spread her ashes. There would be no exhuming of a grave to verify the cause of death.

Her case had seemed open and shut, except that Banner had died a few months later. A heart attack. He was in his fifties and loved cigarettes, greasy food, and booze, according to Gomez. Him having a heart attack wasn't a surprise.

I would have thought it was all coincidental, except I'd remembered her cell phone stuffed in the back of a desk drawer at home. I plugged it in one evening and let it charge. The next morning, I turned it on and discovered several threatening messages from an unknown number. The owner of the number had proved impossible to track down.

Over lunch one afternoon with Gomez and her partner, Phil Moody, she'd told me she would have a forensics tech try to get more off the phone than what I could find. So, I handed the phone to her. That was the last time I saw it. Someone had stolen it from the crime lab.

I did not know what to think. Gomez's theory that Autumn had been murdered now had legs, but the disappearance of the cell phone raised more questions than answers. Could it have been a mistake? I doubted it. Someone had to know it was her phone and was afraid of what forensics might find on it. Gomez wouldn't let me speak to her friend at the lab. She said she had to keep what she did hush hush. She could get in trouble, and there wasn't enough evidence to open a formal investigation.

She had spoken to her contact who said that the phone was gone from where they had stashed it. Poof. Like that.

The threatening messages on Autumn's phone hinted that the sender was someone of power or authority or both. Not likely to be a normal crime scene tech. This told me that whatever happened to Autumn was bigger than I originally thought–which had been nothing.

That was the usual conversation I had with people when

Autumn's name arose, which was rare anymore. Thankfully.

I told none of this to Shelly. She didn't need to know. Besides, that wouldn't answer her original question, as compelling as Autumn's death now seemed to be.

If I could, I'd stop everything to find out who killed her. *If* someone killed her. Unfortunately, I had bills and employees to pay. They counted on me to run the business. Autumn used to have a big hand in that. Now it was left up to me, and I was the idiot who had wanted to expand the business. Sheesh. Garden City Reads, by the way, was being held up by red tape. Fun.

A vivid image still lived in my head. The moment I first saw Autumn. Made me smile every time.

I grinned. "Autumn? She was the best. Had this infectious personality that seemed to draw everyone in. The first time she met someone, anyone, she could make you feel like her best friend. She was engaging and a superb listener. Still the smartest person I've ever known."

"Aww. That's sweet."

"She had strong morals, too. Never swore. Never did drugs. She'd have an occasional glass of red wine, but her personality became bubblier after a few glasses. Other than that, she was straightlaced and the kindest woman I ever met. She possessed a sensitivity and positive outlook on life. Her morals are what drew her to the court system. She was a firm believer in that if you broke the law, you should be punished for it."

The thought stopped me for a moment. Had her conviction that all wrongdoers be punished lead to her murder? I didn't have time to dwell on that. I changed gears and moved on. "She always either had a book in her hand or one nearby. It was her idea to open the bookstore."

"What about you? Did you share her love of books?"

"Not to her level. Yeah, I'll read something every night before I turn out the lights, but I've never been a person to carry a book around everywhere I go, like Autumn."

"I hoped she liked e-readers, otherwise your home would be filled up with books."

"Nope. She liked the feel of a good old-fashioned paperback in her hands. The cases of books she had in the attic helped us stock the store at first. I handled the coffee side of it, one of my true loves, and she did the book side. We hired a couple people to start with, while she continued working at the courthouse. That way, we made enough money to stay afloat. In between, she handled all the paperwork, books, and design of the store. We were almost to where she could quit her job when she passed. It was her baby."

If she were still alive, the store would have been in a position financially for her to leave the courthouse. It saddened me to think that we could have fulfilled our dream of working together at Myrtle Beach Reads. We always pictured me serving coffee behind the counter on one side of the store and looking straight across to see her selling books on the other side. That was our dream together. A dream that would never come to fruition.

"That's sweet. Speaking of babies, did you have any?"

I shook my head. There was only so much I was going to tell this young lady whom I just met. I left out the part about Autumn being pregnant with our first child at the time of her death. We had tried for years to have a baby and finally succeeded. I hadn't known she was pregnant when she died. That came out later when her mom told me that Autumn had confided the news with her before she could tell me. She apparently had a surprise planned for me that weekend to give me the joyous news. That never happened.

I hesitated for a moment to regain my slipping composure. My eyes watered, which I swiped away with one hand. I answered, "No, we didn't. We tried. We were married for a long time but never ended up having a baby."

"Oh, I'm so sorry," Shelly said. She, likewise, used the back of her hand to clear away tears. "Brian and I are planning on having them someday. He wants three."

"What about you? How many do you want?"

"Brian and I are on the same page with that."

"That's great. I wish you the best of success with that."

"Thank you." Her voice hardened. "We have to find him first."

"We will," I said, unsure if I could back up that statement.

"I like that you didn't talk about her looks first," Shelly said. "That's not typical of men. You guys describe their body and/or face first before getting to their personality."

"I'm not your typical guy."

"I suppose not."

"What did she look like?"

Her question made me think of the first time I saw her while we were in college and the last time I saw her before she headed off to work the morning of her death. In my mind, she hadn't aged a bit.

"Let's see," I said. "She was about average height and rakishly thin. It didn't matter what she ate, she never seemed to gain weight."

"I'm jealous," Shelly said, patting her flat stomach. "I always go for a run in the morning and do yoga when I can to work off the fattening food that Brian and I eat for our videos."

"Oh, Autumn was that way too. We rode bikes from our house to the beach about every morning or to the store when we needed to pick up a few things. She had friends she'd meet for yoga classes in Market Common. She stayed active."

"That's good. What else?"

"Her hair was naturally curly, dark brown, and hung down to her shoulders. She had green eyes that mesmerized me. If there was something she wanted, or wanted to do, if she fixed me in her gaze with those eyes, I was powerless. She had that effect on others as well. I know it's cliché, but her smile lit up a room."

"Sounds like a wonderful woman."

"That she was. There will never be another Autumn."

She frowned. "Has it been difficult to move on?"

I gripped the steering wheel tighter. "I'm trying. It's hard. For a while, I was stuck in a rut. Just took one day at a time and moved through life like a robot. I'd get up. Go to work. Come home. Rinse and repeat. Do anything to stay busy. Then, I discovered a dead body one morning, and that kicked me out of it. At that point, I thought I had moved on, but I learned that her death might not have been what I thought."

"What do you mean?"

I took a deep breath. "I learned that someone may have murdered her."

Shelly gasped. "Oh no!"

"And I can't move on until I figure that out."

"How are you going to do that?"

I thought of the obstacles, roadblocks, and time that had passed since her death. There was no trail of evidence. Only conjecture, Gomez's gut feeling, threatening messages, and a stolen cell phone.

"I don't know, but I'm not resting until I do."

CHAPTER
TWELVE

I made a left onto 8th Avenue North into the open area where the old Pavilion used to be. Now, there was a zip line setup, an empty field, and sandy beach volleyball courts separating 8th and 9th Avenues. Traffic backed up. I waited for the line of cars to move. When they finally puttered ahead, the brake lights of a vehicle parked in front of Nathan's Hot Dogs flared. I stopped and flashed my lights, letting them know I'd wait for them to back out. They did, and I took their spot.

"That was easy," I said. "It's hard to find a spot this close to the Boardwalk this time of night on a Saturday evening."

"Great," Shelly said and opened her door.

"Has Izzy responded?"

She checked her phone. "Not yet."

After exiting the Jeep, I joined her on the sidewalk. We walked to the Ocean Boulevard intersection. Crowds of tourists bunched up on the concrete, wandering aimlessly. Many were there for the experience. Ambient light from the businesses lining the oceanfront cast a glow on the ocean. There weren't any spotlights shining on the water to protect any nesting sea turtles.

During this time of year, the Boardwalk became a melting pot of cultures from across the country and the world. People spoke languages I couldn't identify and dressed in vibrant beach outfits. Business at the bookstore increased as well. Winona and I were scheduled to open the store at noon tomorrow. I hadn't figured out how I would juggle that with not knowing what would happen with Shelly between now and then.

If I needed to, I could operate on a few hours of sleep, as I did the day after Hurricane Karen trapped us in John Allen Howard's seaside mansion on the Golden Mile last fall. Then again, I fell asleep at my desk.

I didn't know where this night would take us, but Brian's disappearance piqued my interest. Something about his actions today and leading up to it bugged me. They reminded me of something I couldn't quite place. I had already voiced one side of what I thought Brian was up to, but my gut told me there was more to it.

I hated to see a young woman like Shelly all alone so far from home who had no clue what to do. The chivalrous side of me had to help.

We crossed 8th Avenue at the light and headed toward the main part of the Boardwalk where Ripley's Believe-It-Or-Not Museum, Peaches Corner, and the Bowery faced us. The bright neon lights of the Sky Wheel loomed overhead behind them as the wheel spun in a slow arc. My friend Marilyn owned a comic bookstore called We Have Issues near The Gay Dolphin.

The evening was crisp and sticky. Normal for the end of May. A cooler than usual winter gave way, with a vengeance, to a blazing spring.

Grub N' Go Eats was located a block into the promenade, on the same side as the Bowery. We waited again at the 9th Avenue stoplight to cross. Shelly hadn't said a word since we got out of the Jeep. Instead, she craned her neck, studying every face, trying to find Brian.

I just realized that I didn't know exactly what he looked like. My only sight of him was the side of his face when we spotted him in Conway. There were a few scattered men and boys in my sight right now either with blond or curly hair and glasses. None of them caught Shelly's attention, so I assumed they weren't Brian.

"Do you have a picture of Brian?" I asked.

"Hmm. Yeah." She pulled a phone from out of her pocketbook, lit the screen, and tapped a few buttons. "Here he is. He was always more camera shy before this trip, but now that we've done dozens of videos, he wants me to take all the pictures of him I can."

She handed me her phone. The picture was a selfie of Brian and Shelly. He held the phone out with one hand. His other arm was wrapped around her shoulders. They both wore big smiles. His hair was on the bushy side, as was the beard he wore. The facial hair obscured a paunchy jawline. He wore silver wire-rimmed glasses.

I handed the phone back to her. "Got it. Thanks."

A family of six skirted past us on their way to the Sky Wheel. The kids yelling at their parents to go faster. Shelly looked at me with a bemused smile on her face.

My shoulders bounced. We had to speak louder to hear each other. "What can I say? People love it here."

"What about you?"

I glanced around the pressing crowds. The aromas of hot dogs and popcorn were killing me. The empty carbs from the cookies didn't last long. "I like it better during the mornings when it's not so busy."

"Sounds reasonable."

The only thing about coming to this area of the Boardwalk during the mornings was that its newest and most popular restaurant, Grub N' Go Eats, didn't open until noon. It was the antithesis of a breakfast restaurant. Of all the variety of restaurants in Myrtle Beach, breakfast establishments were the most common. You could eat at a different one every day for almost a year without going to the same place twice.

Speaking of different, that was in Grub N' Go's blood. They were a breakfast place that wasn't open during breakfast and stayed open until well past midnight, even after some of the area bars closed. People staggering back to their hotels or cars could stop in at Grub N' Go to get a cup of strong coffee and a thick breakfast burrito to sober up before leaving the area.

The restaurant blended in with its surroundings. A hungry person could enter the place from two sides, one on Ocean Boulevard, the other on the wooden promenade facing the ocean. On a normal morning, if you drove or walked past the place, it would blend in with its surroundings. A muted yellow Grub N' Go sign hung on the brick wall that rose above the sidewalk-spanning awning. The window displayed a sign that read "2 Burritos for $12." That was it.

But, if you came any time between half an hour before Grub N' Go opened to well after midnight, you would find a line of people waiting to get in. On both sides. As we did now.

We got in line and people watched while we waited. Every time someone exited the restaurant, the next in line would enter. We were about ten feet from the door when it opened and a trim man with premature silver hair and designer eyeglasses stepped out, looked once in our direction, and walked the other way down the sidewalk.

Shelly gasped.

"What is it?" I asked.

She pointed. "That man. I think I know him."

"The guy that just came out?"

"Yeah him."

The line moved, and we took a step forward. We watched as he mixed in with the tourists and receded from view.

"Know him from where?"

"I think he works for Brian's dad. That's quite a coincidence."

The hair pricked up on the back of my neck. "I hate coincidences. There is never a coincidence when a mystery is involved."

"What do you mean?"

I tapped my foot on the sidewalk. How best to explain this in a short amount of time? Which is all we had. "I'm not a person who believes in predestination. That everything happens for a reason determined by an entity way before you're born. I look at everything from a statistical perspective. The Law of Truly Large Numbers."

"What is that?"

"That in large populations, any weird event can happen. Like, let's say you go on vacation to Brazil and meet someone you don't know who is from your hometown in Louisiana."

"That's a coincidence," Shelly said.

"No," I corrected. "That's a statistical probability. If you drilled down to it, there's a formula you could come up with to explain how two people who live close together in one place end up in a different part of the world at the same time."

"Okay. How does that relate here?"

"That man who might work with Brian's dad being almost a thousand miles from home and here in Myrtle Beach, on this night a few hours after Brian ditched you at a place of business owned by one of his friends can't be a coincidence. The odds would be astronomical. There's a reason he's here."

Shelly needed no more convincing. She took off down the sidewalk after him, her high heels clicking with each step. I broke the line and followed her. Tourists stopped in their tracks at the sight of me chasing after Shelly and shouted in exclamation at the scene we were causing.

As we passed by the front door of Mad Myrtle's Ice Creamery, two very large and powerful arms owned by two large and very imposing men stopped me in my tracks.

"Whoa, whoa there fella," a man with a deep voice said. "Just where do you think you're going?"

I struggled in their grasp, but it was no use. Their grips were like a vise. I wasn't going anywhere as long as these two men held me. People gathered around us but kept their distance.

"Let go of me! He's getting away!" I shouted.

In a calm voice like that of a hostage negotiator, the man said, "Looked like you were chasing after that girl. We ain't having that."

I turned to look at my captors for the first time. Shelly and the mystery man were out of my sight. I wouldn't know where to go even if they released me.

The two men wore the uniforms of the Myrtle Beach Police Department. Their badges glinted in the phosphorescent lights. One had light skin. The hostage negotiator with the deep voice had dark skin. Neither was to be messed with.

"Look," I explained, after we had a moment to catch our breaths, "that girl is my friend. She's chasing after someone who might know why her fiancé went missing."

The officers shared a look. One said, "You're going to explain that to us."

They released their grasp on me and told the crowd to break it up. They led me to a narrow alley next to Grub N' Go. At least it was well-lit. There was nothing I could do for Shelly now. They'd catch me if I tried to run after her and wouldn't be as gentle as they were before. If you could call it that. I'd be fortunate not to end up in the back of a squad car headed back to the precinct. The best thing now was for me to keep my cool so they would keep theirs.

"I wasn't chasing after that woman," I explained.

"That's what it looked like to us," said the dark-skinned officer. His badge identified him as "Battles."

"Yeah," the other one agreed. His badge read "Dame."

I explained the situation, starting from the beginning when I first saw Shelly. When I reached the present and them grabbing me, Dame said, "And you say she called the police?"

"Yeah," I answered. "They said they couldn't do anything yet. For her to wait it out."

The two officers looked at each other and back at me. Battles said, "You're Clark, right?"

"I am."

"Helped us out a few times, right?"

"I did."

Dame and Battles shared another look. "You know Detectives Gomez and Moody, right?"

"I do. It's been a while since I've spoken to either of them,"

I said.

"I know they're busy this weekend. Been some chaos going on with all the travelers being in town. They're up to their necks in it."

"That's why I haven't called them," I said. "Right now, we're pursuing a trail on Brian. We've been following it all evening and were hoping to catch him at Grub N' Go."

"But you were running away from there." Dame said.

I nodded. "Right. Brian and the guy who owns the restaurant used to be college buddies. This was the last place Shelly and I had to go to try to find Brian. We were hoping to find some answers here when she saw the guy that she thinks works with Brian's dad."

"Ah," they said in unison.

At that time, Shelly walked past the alleyway. Her head moved in all directions except for ours. She didn't see us. I shouted, "Shelly!"

She stopped and came back. The two officers and I stood perhaps five feet into the alley. She put a hand on her chest which moved up and down as she tried to catch her breath. "Clark! I didn't see you there." Then she looked at the MBPD officers. "Hello."

Battles grabbed my arm and squeezed. The man could bend steel with that grip. I'd have bruises tomorrow. In a voice deep enough to send a tremor down the promenade, Battles asked, "Is this man bothering you?"

Shelly's eyebrows went in two different directions. "No. He's been helping me all evening."

Battles let go of me and said, "That's what he told us. We wanted to make sure he was telling the truth."

"He is," Shelly said, drawing closer. "He's been my savior today. I don't know what I would have done without him."

"What is your name?" Dame asked.

I had already told them her name, so I figured Dame was verifying.

Her hands shook and her cheeks were still red from the exertion. She held her set of heels between two fingers of one hand. The two-inch heel on one shoe was hanging on by a thread. She breathed out. "Shelly. Shelly Garland."

"Clark tells us that your fiancé is missing," Battles said.

Her head tipped forward. "Yes."

"Clark filled us in on everything," Dame said.

She looked all three of us in the eyes, one by one. The whites were visible in hers. Her hands still shook. I could tell she was reaching a breaking point.

"Did you catch him?"

"No," she said, the disgust clear in her voice. "I got close enough to shout his name."

"Was it him?" I asked. "Did he hear you?"

Her lips twisted together. "Don't think so. It was him. I'm sure of it, but he disappeared."

CHAPTER
THIRTEEN

Officers Battles and Dame held us in the alley for nearly half an hour, putting us through what they called "investigative detention." They grilled Shelly. They grilled me. Separately on opposite ends of the alley, then took our information and Brian's for good measure.

All the while, Brian got farther away, as did the mystery man Shelly chased after. At least I had some food in my stomach.

When they let us go, all of us exited the alley. They went one way. Shelly and I went back to Grub N' Go.

"Do you think they'll do anything with what we told them?" Shelly asked as we took position in line. This time, we started a little closer to the door.

I turned to look at Battles and Dame as they resumed their patrol. Their backs were to us. Dame said something that caused Battles to tilt his head back and laugh. Probably about me being old enough to be Shelly's dad and trying to chase her down.

"Nah, I think they got our stories to cover their behinds in case something happens down the road."

"Like what?"

"That I abduct you. Then they can look back at their notes and say that you covered for me. That they didn't see any reason to bring out the handcuffs and allowed us to go on our merry way."

"I imagine they have more important matters to attend to."

At this time of night, the Boardwalk was still a zoo. People of all ages and types roamed around.

"I'm sure you're right." The couple in front of us entered. A hearty aroma wafted from the opening. Despite the pound of cookie digesting in my stomach, it rumbled. We were next in line to enter. "I didn't get to hear what you said to the cops. Who was that guy that came out of here?"

"I'm not sure what his name is. Curtis, maybe. I've seen him around the home office of Gator's Landing. I think he's on the board of directors."

My mind tried to connect the dots, but there wasn't enough information floating around up there to do it. Yet.

I said, "I didn't get too good of a look at him. If it is this Curtis guy, how old is he?"

"He's older. Older than you, I think."

"Okay." I tried to imagine a thread between Brian, Dwayne Clayton, and Curtis. Brian knew Dwayne from college and Curtis from his dad's business. "Did Curtis know Dwayne? Are they related?"

"No clue. It's a small town where we come from. Could be."

"Like, Curtis isn't Dwayne's dad or anything?"

"No. Dwayne's dad is a lawyer. I know him and his mom. I know little about Curtis other than he works with Brian's dad. What could he be doing here?"

The door opened. A family walked out with bags of food and drinks in hand. I held open the door for them to exit and for Shelly to enter.

I said, "Let's go inside and see what we can see."

* * *

Because the building that housed Grub N' Go was an older one, Dwayne Clayton had done his best to make the interior look brand new. Beyond the smells of frying bacon, sausage, and chorizo, the dining area hinted at that "old building smell."

My stomach grumbled.

Like when any new business opens on the Boardwalk, I make it a point to seek out and meet the new owners. When I was a member of the Myrtle Beach Downtown Development Corporation two years ago, part of my role was to get the business owners and various governmental departments to work together. Then I got caught in a restricted area late one night at the OceanScapes Resort. I resigned from that role shortly thereafter.

Dwayne Clayton's ownership and my time on the board overlapped by a year. I met Dwayne once, welcomed him to the area, offered any help he might need in making ties with the local business community, and invited him to a meeting. Besides thanking me for welcoming him and his business, he declined my other offers. He made it clear that he was here for one thing: to run his business and make money. My subtle suggestions that a rising tide lifts all boats fell upon deaf ears. He handed me a free breakfast burrito and sent me on my merry way.

To his credit, business seemed to boom, despite not making acquaintances with other Boardwalk business owners. When I visited my friend Marilyn's comic book shop in the afternoon and evenings, I had to veer around hungry eaters lined up outside of Grub N' Go's doors. Maybe he didn't need our help after all.

Two lines stretched from doors located on the oceanfront side and Ocean Boulevard entrances and met in the middle at two cash registers. Grub N' Go had a narrow space on the Boardwalk. There were no tables inside, only a line of barstools and a bar that spanned the restaurant from one end to the other. As Shelly and I set foot inside, most spots were taken.

Grub N' Go's claim to fame was the "Go" part of their name. They offered all manner of breakfast burritos, filled almost to the point of bursting their rolled tortilla containers. They made one of those fancy burrito chain restaurants look like something off the kid's menu. Since they installed the Boardwalk, hot dogs, corn dogs, and hamburgers were the popular hand-held choices for tourists strolling the downtown. With the addition of Grub N' Go, burritos ate into much of that space.

As we got closer, I saw that none other than Dwayne Clayton himself was busy running a register. It amazed me that on this Saturday night, three of the four restaurant owners we sought happened to be working. This was a holiday weekend, after all. I figured that when the money is rolling in, it's better to have the boss in the house to make sure everything ran well.

A line of griddles stood behind the counter, reminding me of a Waffle House. Two cooks were busy slicing, dicing, and grilling a bevy of meats and toppings. The aroma was killing me.

If it weren't for Shelly, I'd be sitting on my back deck overlooking Lake Vivian, drenched in mosquito spray, and sipping on an old-fashioned with an old Zac Brown Band album playing through outdoor speakers. I trusted my employees to run the bookstore even on the busiest of days. Since I solved the first murder, I'd spent less and less time selling books. When I was in the store, I spent my time running the coffee bar (my true love) and writing books. Well, one book at least. The feedback from readers from the first book was positive enough to drive me to write a second book. I had a series planned, loosely based on some of my past sleuthing capers.

Now that we were here, and the smell and look of the burritos told the cookies in my stomach to hurry and vacate to make room, Dwayne Clayton soon stood in front of us. For the customers before us, he was cordial and kept a smile on his face. When we stepped to the front, his expression changed.

When he looked at Shelly, his eyes widened. A vein popped out on the side of his neck. He mumbled something to himself and looked back at the busy employees behind him, maybe looking for one of them to take over. Although he looked like a man ready to escape, the smile remained, but the hardening of his expression belied his grin.

Then he looked at me. Perspiration broke out on his forehead.

"Hi Dwayne," Shelly said.

"Hey, Shelly," he said through his teeth.

"Remember me?" I said.

He nodded. "I do. Clark, right?"

"That's it." No sense beating around the bush to a man who looked like a rabbit ready to scurry underneath it. "Have you seen Brian McConnell here this evening?"

His mouth twitched. "N-no, I haven't."

"Look, he abandoned Shelly alongside the road in Conway this afternoon. We've been following in his tracks since then, going to various restaurants where he and Shelly had done food reviews over the last two weeks. This is the last one."

He looked at Shelly. "Oh, he left you?"

There wasn't a trace of surprise in his voice.

Thinking back on this evening's adventure, we should have come here and waited after going to Big Hoggz. Despite the argument that broke out between Brian and Dwayne following the video review, they were still friends who had a history together from two-thousand miles away. When you're in a strange land, you seek the familiar. Sometimes the familiar can help, or it can lead to danger.

Judging from Dwayne's body language and speech, I sensed the latter. Now, I needed to figure out what it meant. My first thought was that he had done something to Brian. Then I remembered the mystery man.

I asked, "What about a man named Curtis? We saw him leaving here half an hour to forty-five minutes ago. Maybe a little older than me. Head of gray hair. That ring a bell?"

Dwayne's eyebrows tried to escape his forehead. "N-no. Don't recall anyone like that."

Shelly had had enough. Her nostrils flared and her lips curled as she balled her fists and pounded on the counter. All the noise faded. Everyone stopped to look at the commotion. "You're lying! We just saw him leave here!"

Dwayne's mouth opened. He backed up a step. He held his hands out. "Look, Shelly, I don't know what you're talking about. I swear. You're causing a scene." He stamped his foot and pointed to the door. "I'm going to ask you and your friend to leave."

To my outright dismay, Shelly said, "Not a chance."

The entire diner hung on every word. The three of us knew how this looked.

I could have piled on but chose to be the voice of reason. "Look Dwayne, why don't we step into the back and talk like calm adults? We can sort this out. Shelly is scared to death right now that Brian is leaving her or is in trouble. You know more than what you're telling us, and you know it."

Dwayne couldn't speak. Right now, his employees saw weakness emanating from their owner. The only way to de-escalate the scene was to follow my suggestion. He realized that and looked at one worker who was busy collecting trash. "Andres! Come back here and run the register for a few minutes."

A tan-skinned boy no older than a teenager jerked his head around from his trash duties, looked at Dwayne, and then at the line. "*S-si, senor.*"

Dwayne lifted a section of the counter for Shelly and me to pass through. Andres followed.

As the diners went back to their food, noise in the diner resumed. The show was over.

"This way." Dwayne shook his head in annoyance before pushing open a silver door with a small square window near the top, then ushered us into the back.

I held the door open for Shelly to walk through after Dwayne. Perhaps we'd finally get some answers.

CHAPTER
FOURTEEN

The back room held a long prep station, two refrigerators, and a freezer door. Three people busied themselves preparing various toppings for the burritos. Several food safety posters lined the walls. Over time, posters like these became more of a legality decoration than truly followed suggestions for effective protocol. The workers looked up when we entered.

He looked at them and jerked his head at the door we just came through. They got the message, dropped what they were doing, washed their hands, and scampered out.

When they were gone, Dwayne motioned us to follow him to his office, past the refrigerators and freezer. The door had a sign stating that the freezer was broken and not to open the door. That shouldn't be a problem, since part of their modus operandi was that their food was fresh and never frozen.

The door to the office stood open, revealing a cluttered desk and several file cabinets. He led us in before moving a stack of file boxes so he could close the door.

Two chairs sat before his desk. Shelly sat. I remained standing. I would not get comfortable and let him believe he could smooth talk his way around this.

He collapsed into his chair. It squeaked in protest. He wasn't a heavy man, but the seat had seen better days. He ran a hand along the side of his jaw. "Sorry for the mess."

"Looks like my office," I said. If it threw up.

Shelly cut to the chase. "Have you seen Brian?"

"No."

I said, "We know you've seen Curtis. We saw him leave, and you were up front taking orders. You lying to us?"

"I was."

"Why?" Shelly said.

"I don't know. I panicked."

"What did Curtis want?" I asked.

"The same thing you and Shelly did. He was looking for Brian."

I crossed my arms. "Did you know who he was?"

He hesitated a split second. "No. Never seen him before."

Shelly looked up and back at me. We both thought the same thing.

"I don't think you're being truthful," Shelly said.

The cramped office was warm enough to begin with. The pressure Shelly and I were putting on Dwayne had sweat beading across his brow. I saw the look in his eyes. One of being placed in an untenable position. I knew why.

I said, "Shelly told me about your relationship with Brian. You go way back. He and her went on this cross-country food tour that was scheduled to end with this stop in Myrtle Beach." I jabbed my index finger at the top of his desk to punctuate my point. I raised my voice, and as I did, I kept poking my finger on his desk with every sentence. "They scheduled eight stops during their stay here. Half go like normal, then he goes crazy over the last half of them. All our travels this evening brought us to you.

Then we get here, and we see some dude that works with his dad two-thousand miles away. It's late. I'm hungry. I'm tired. I'm grumpy. I want to go home and go to bed. You're all that is standing in the way. Tell us what is going on or I'm going to call my friends from the MBPD."

The whites of his eyes showed. Perspiration dripped down his face. It beaded up on the back of my neck as well.

Dwayne's green eyes flitted between the two of us as he weighed what to say next. The ball was in his court. To further nail down my threat, I took out my phone and lit the screen.

He held out both hands in surrender. "Okay. Okay. I'll tell you what's going on. You gotta promise to not tell Brian where this came from. I don't want this coming back on me."

"Deal," I said without consulting Shelly. If there was any criminal activity involved, I would report it to Gomez. That wasn't part of Dwayne's deal. He said nothing about not telling the police.

He held out his hands in a placating gesture. "Look, seeing that guy wasn't as crazy as it looks."

"How is that?" Shelly said.

Dwayne looked at her and said, "Brian's dad sent him to see me."

"Sent him to see you? Why?" I said.

Dwayne sat forward in his chair. "He was checking up on Brian."

"Why would he need to do that?"

He gave me a patronizing look. "Do you have kids?"

Every time someone asked me that question, my heart fell. This wasn't the time to explain to him the reason, so I said, "I do not."

"I do," he said, pointing at his chest. "Twin girls. Both are in elementary school. I get worried every time I send them to school, when I know that they'll come home that afternoon. It's part of my being. If they go stay overnight at a friend's house, I get worried when I know all they're doing is playing games, eating junk food, and staying up too late." He focused on Shelly. "Now, imagine one of your kids decides they're going to load up in a small RV and travel across the country. Wouldn't you be worried sick?"

Shelly's head dipped. "I speak to my parents every day."

"What about Brian?" I asked.

"I'm not sure," she said. "I don't think he calls them. He sends them text messages, I think."

"The guy that came in here," Dwayne said, "said that Brian's dad hadn't heard from him in six months."

Dwayne's statement sucked the air out of the room and Shelly. Her chest heaved with deep breaths. She rocked her head. Something in my brain *pinged*.

"I can't, can't believe that," she said after a moment. Her hands shook. Muted voices murmured through the walls from the dining room. "My parents and his don't speak together much, but I'm sure his dad might have mentioned something to them at some point. I know Brian's dad watches our videos because we see his name pop up in liked video notifications."

Dwayne opened his hands. "Don't know what to tell you. That's what the guy said."

"Why did he come to see you at this time of night?" I said.

Dwayne directed his attention to me while Shelly gathered herself. "You'd have to ask him. All I know is he waited in line like you did, and then introduced himself. He knew who I was, even though I'd never seen him before in my life. Said he worked with Brian's dad, and he was trying to connect with him. He asked me if I had seen him."

"Had you?" I asked.

His Adam's apple bobbed. "I did the other day when he and Shelly came for the review."

"Ah," I said. "She tells me you and Brian had some strong words with each other. What was that about, if you don't mind me asking?"

He bit the corner of his lip and glanced at Shelly. "It goes back to college."

"What does?"

He let out a puff of air as his shoulders deflated. "Look, I might as well tell you, Shelly."

"Tell me what?"

"It was me that started it the other day. Not Brian."

"Oh." She scratched the side of her head. "I thought it was him."

"No, it wasn't." He stared at her and ignored me. He seemed to weigh his next statement carefully. "This is going to hurt, but when Brian told me you and him were getting married, I told him something."

Without realizing it, both Shelly and I leaned forward. Her arms were crossed.

Shelly balled her fists. "What did you say?"

He gulped, then said, "I told him he could do better than you."

CHAPTER
FIFTEEN

I wanted to lunge across the desk and grab Dwayne by the collar. I didn't need to. Shelly acted.

Like a lion leaping while hunting prey, Shelly sprang from her chair, reached across, and slapped Dwayne across the face as hard as she could. I edged forward and readied myself in case he retaliated.

"How dare you!" Shelly yelled in a volume that I didn't think was possible for a woman of her size. If we could hear voices coming through the office walls, I'm sure the people on the other side heard her too.

Dwayne rubbed his reddening jaw and worked his chin from side to side. He looked from her to me. I'm not the most physically imposing guy, but I was bigger than Dwayne. I'd never been in a fight before, but he didn't know that.

"C'mon, Shelly," Dwayne said, holding out a hand. "We go way back. Known each other since college."

She returned to her chair. "Yes, I know," she bit out. "You were always this hoity-toity rich kid born with a silver spoon in your mouth with a chip on your shoulder. I don't come from a wealthy family like you, and you always looked down on me for it."

"I will not argue with you. I just know that Brian had chances to get with girls who were, you know…" He failed to find a proper word to complete the sentence that didn't result in a slap on the other cheek.

I finished it for him. "You mean girls who came from a wealthier pedigree?"

He looked up at me. "Yes."

"You jerk," Shelly said. "You always were one. Always will be."

"Look, I'm trying here," he said. "I have my business, a wife, twins, and a mortgage. Life hit hard after college. My parents gave me the money to buy this place and moved to Europe. My wife's parents retired to Hawaii."

"And now you have to worry about money for the first time in your life." The rushing sound in my ears dissipated as did the tension in the room. I sat down beside Shelly.

"Yes. I'll admit, I wasn't prepared for it," he said. "I work my butt off here. Especially since Covid and the staffing issues we've had. I'm here six days a week." He blinked. "No, seven this week. One of my two cashiers called out this evening. I was supposed to have been home with the wife and kids but ended up having to work the front instead."

I couldn't relate. Everyone except for Humphrey had perfect attendance at the bookstore. I didn't have to rely on unreliable teenagers to run the store.

"Is it a pay week?" I asked.

"Yep," Dwayne answered. "These kids get some money in their pockets and don't think they have to work for a few days. They don't realize that it hurts them on the next one."

"No, thinking two weeks ahead isn't something most teens do. They're focused on the weekend or on what they're going to do after high school. Not what happens in the interim."

"Well said." Dwayne lowered his brow. "You are as perceptive as they say."

I spread my hands. "Can't help it. Let's get back to the subject at hand. If you're as short-staffed as you claim you are, then I'm sure you want to wrap this up and get back out there."

He tilted his head. "I do."

I crossed my arms. "You and Brian got into it because you told him Shelly wasn't good enough for him."

"I've been telling him that since I met him."

Shelly's face glowed. Her small hands balled into fists. I touched her wrist to calm her. She relaxed.

I said, "And he defended Shelly, didn't he?"

Dwayne looked at her and said, "He did. Vehemently. Told me they were made for each other, and he wouldn't hear anything to the contrary."

"That's my man," Shelly said.

"He ended our friendship on the spot," Dwayne said. "Haven't seen him since."

Shelly smiled to herself.

"And this Curtis guy hadn't seen him either?" I asked.

Dwayne shook his head. "Don't guess so."

I tilted my head to the side. Shelly and I nodded to each other. We were done here. I was sure she'd be happy if she never had to see Dwayne Clayton again. I felt the same way. The feeling was probably mutual.

"Thanks for your time," I said and stood.

"No problem," he said and turned to Shelly. "Look, I'm sorry if I hurt your feelings, but I'm just telling you what caused our argument."

Shelly opened her mouth to say something but didn't.

Instead, she turned and stomped out of the office without a word. Her heels clacked on the floor with each step.

"Have a good evening," I said and followed her out.

"You too," he said from his seat.

I closed the office door as I left and watched as Shelly exited the kitchen, back out to the front. I lagged. As I tried to assimilate what we learned from Dwayne, something about this back room bothered me. Something Shelly had mentioned earlier. I looked all around and tried to remember what was odd about this room.

Then it hit me. The freezer. Shelly had said everything at Grub N' Go was made fresh, never frozen.

As Dwayne opened his door to follow me out, I passed by the freezer door. Reaching out, I grasped the cool silver handle and pulled.

The door opened along with the vapors of cold air followed by a body falling out and toppling to the floor with a *thump*.

I groaned. "Oh no. Not again."

CHAPTER
SIXTEEN

The body was wrapped in butcher's paper. It fell like it had been leaning against the freezer door. Thankfully, there was no sign of blood, meaning that the person hadn't been actually butchered. Blood thundered through my ears. My eyes bulged. I had to force myself to blink.

Behind me, Dwayne screamed in a high-pitched voice, reminiscent of Fay Wray, when she first laid eyes on King Kong in the classic movie.

As calmly as I could, I said to him, "Call 911."

He nodded dumbly and left me alone with the dead person. Bile rose in the back of my throat.

I had a flashback to when I first discovered the body of Paige Whitaker rolled up in a rug behind Myrtle Beach Reads. There, I peeled back the rug just enough to see who it was and the cause of death.

Shelly and some other workers barged through the kitchen door after hearing Dwayne scream.

One of the workers, a reed-thin young man with scraggly hair escaping his Grub N' Go hat let out a yell like Dwayne's upon seeing the body. He ran out of the kitchen, screaming, "Dead body! Dead body!"

His voice receded, accompanied by a cacophony of shouts and feet pounding the floors in the dining room.

Shelly reappeared, saw the body, and held her hands over her mouth, unable to speak, eyes wide.

The other worker who came in the door with Shelly was a plump woman. Her hair was pulled back in a fluffy ball. She chewed some gum and popped a bubble while looking at the body with disinterest.

She bobbed her head up and down. "That's no good," she said before exiting through the kitchen door.

I held up a hand to Shelly to hold her at bay and to let her know I had things under control. Which was debatable.

The victim was not tall. Long hair from around the head escaped through openings in the layers of butcher paper. I found a dry dishcloth by a nearby sink basin. I grabbed it and reached out toward the head and used the cloth to grasp the paper and peeled it back, revealing a woman with blonde hair. She looked to be in her twenties and bared a striking resemblance to Shelly. I didn't want to peel back the paper too much so as not to disturb any evidence. There wasn't an obvious cause of death. I placed the paper back over her the way I found it and put the dishcloth back where I found it.

"It's not Brian," I told her.

She let out a relieved breath. "Oh, thank God. Who is it?"

"I don't know yet." I returned my attention to the victim. "What are you doing here?"

I was glad she didn't answer back. If she had, I would have screamed a scream that would have put Dwayne's to shame.

Dwayne returned. His hands and body shook. He kept a good distance between us and the body.

"Do you know who this is?" I asked.

He took a step closer and leaned forward. He squinted and said in a trembling voice, "That's Christi. Christi Hunter. She works here."

Shelly took the courage to come closer. "Wait, she was one of the people hired to be our body doubles in the videos."

Dwayne's chin dipped. "And a fine worker at that."

"Was she working today?" I asked.

He rubbed a hand over his mouth. Couldn't take his eyes off her. "No. She was supposed to be off. I haven't seen her since Thursday."

"How often do people go in this freezer?"

"Not very often. There's not much in there. Fresh. Never frozen, remember?"

I nodded and looked back at the victim.

"Has she worked here for very long?" I asked.

"She hasn't. She worked back here in the kitchen. Could chop meats and veggies with the best of them. I hired her and Tommy around the same time."

"Who's Tommy?"

"A busboy."

"Is he here today?"

"No."

"You say you hired both of them at the same time?"

Something seemed to connect in that brain of his. His eyes brightened. "I did. When Brian told me he was coming to film here, he wanted me to find and hire two people who looked similar to him and Shelly."

"Why?"

"He said something about having them serve as body doubles

in stock footage or something. Like, they'd have their backs to the camera while eating."

Shelly crossed her arms. "I knew nothing about it until we got here."

"That's odd." I looked at Shelly. "If Brian wanted for you and him to be in a shot, why not have someone else hold the camera?"

"Dunno. Brian always was a control freak. Maybe he wanted to make sure the scene was shot right."

"Did Brian come back here at any time after filming and your argument? Tell the truth." I pointed at the body. "This doesn't look good on you."

His Adam's apple bobbed. "I know. Yes, Brian did come here."

"Why?"

"He said maybe he might invest some money into the business and open another location. Wanted to scope the place out when no one was around to get a good sense of the place."

"Good sense?" I said. "*That* doesn't make much sense. What would make sense would be coming in here tonight like Shelly and I did and seeing the long lines going out both doors. That's all the proof of concept I'd need. Looks like you're doing great here."

"Thank you."

I stared at him for another moment. Before I could ask another question, Battles and Dame burst through the door, followed by Detectives Gomez and Moody.

Dwayne backed away into a corner. I stood up from the body and raised my hands to show I didn't have blood on them or a murder weapon.

Gomez wore a purple blouse, a short skirt, and dainty shoes

instead of one of her signature navy pantsuits. For a time, that was how I usually saw her, except for one time during the Paige Whitaker case. Then I saw her in a ravishing green dress the night of a gala at the Chapin Art Museum, and I haven't looked at her the same way since. The downside of that was that I hadn't seen much of her in the months since the death on the Golden Mile. She had a boyfriend, and I hadn't discovered any dead bodies (until now) since then. There wasn't much of a reason for us to be in contact since that morning at the Howard mansion.

Her current outfit would no doubt bounce around my brain a few times.

"Clark," she said. "Why am I not surprised to see you here?"

I tilted my head and shrugged my left shoulder. "We really need to stop meeting like this. Unfortunately, if there's a death on the Boardwalk, they seem to happen around me."

Gomez and her partner, Phil Moody, shared a look with Battles and Dame.

In his gruff voice, Moody said, "You'd be surprised what you don't see around here."

"I bet I would, nor do I want to know," I said.

Dwayne stepped forward. "Hi, I'm Dwayne Clayton. I own this place."

He held out a hand, but none of them made a move to shake it. He dropped it to his side after a moment like a shamed puppy.

Moody came to where I stood beside the body. I stepped aside to allow him free access. The space in front of the freezer where she fell was cramped, and I had to stand in Dwayne's office doorway while Moody stooped over the body.

Battles took up a spot by the door leading from the kitchen to the dining room. Dame crossed to the end of a hall and opened a door leading to a back alley. The same one where they questioned me earlier. He looked both ways and came back, shutting the door behind him.

"No one back there," he said to Gomez.

"Good," she replied. "Go and get any of the customers still in the building to leave. Let's shut this down. Take names, though. Hold the employees. We'll need to question them. Lock the doors. No one enters. No one leaves."

"Roger," he said, and exited the kitchen, moving past Battles.

Gomez motioned me to come to her.

When I got close, I asked, "Did we pull you from a date tonight?"

Her eyes widened. "Yes. How did you know?"

"Your outfit and perfume," I said, "and your makeup is a little heavier than when you're on duty. You look . . . nice."

She touched the side of her face. "Very observant."

"I try."

"For your information, yes, I was on a date."

"Sorry for pulling you out of it." As I said those words, it occurred to me that might not have been the honest thing to say. Truth be told, I've thought about her frequently since that night at the gala. We had a great time, and I thought she was into me. However, the reason I was with her that night was because she had broken up with her boyfriend and needed a date for the evening. They got back together afterward. What was I to do?

"No problem," she said, pulled out a pen and notebook, and then pointed to the body. "Duty calls. Explain to me what happened. Start from the beginning."

Shelly's lips stayed tightly closed. Dwayne stared at a corner of the ceiling.

I took a deep breath and started, "This afternoon, I was sitting at a stoplight in Conway on my way back from a book signing in Marion and saw Shelly screaming into her phone in a mobile home dealer parking lot. She was by herself and looked very distressed. I pulled around the corner and into the lot and asked Shelly what was the matter."

Gomez crossed her arms and looked Shelly up and down. "That's, um, noble of you." To Shelly, "Why were you in that parking lot?"

She opened her mouth, closed it while her eyebrows grew together, then said, "My fiancé, Brian McConnell, left me at a coffee shop a few blocks away. When he didn't come back after a while, I started walking aimlessly toward Myrtle Beach. I was numb. Didn't know what to do."

"Would have been a long walk," Moody said.

Gomez gave him a cross look and turned back to Shelly. "You poor girl. Has he done this before?"

"No. Never," Shelly replied. "We're food bloggers on YouTube. We've been traveling the country for the past year, popping in on cool restaurants and featuring them on our channel. Myrtle Beach was our last stop before we were to go on a cruise, leaving out of Charleston. Then we were supposed to go home to Louisiana."

"So, you were here, far away from home, and he left you stranded?" Gomez asked.

"Yes. Then Clark came to my rescue."

For the first time since entering Grub N' Go, Gomez smiled in my direction. "That's Clark for you. Then what?"

"Brian was supposed to take over his dad's restaurant business." Shelly shifted on the balls of her feet. I'm sure they had to be tired and sore from wearing those heels all day. Until she broke one chasing the mystery man. She had ripped the other heel off and now stood on uneven shoes. "His dad financed our trip as a way of letting Brian have his adventure before diving headfirst into the family business."

Shelly told Gomez about the sudden change in Brian's demeanor over the past few days.

"After we finished our last scheduled review at a place in Conway and were heading back to our campground for the evening, we stopped at a coffee shop. I went to the bathroom. He was gone when I came out. Vanished. I waited for a while to see if he'd come back before leaving and walked down the sidewalk. I decided he wasn't coming back and called 911."

Gomez took this in. "And the dispatcher told you there was nothing they could do until he'd been missing for twenty-four hours, correct?"

"Yes," Shelly answered. "Unless he was a danger to himself or others."

We relayed the details of our journey up and down the Grand Strand, searching out various restaurant owners whom Brian had conflicts with and how they led them to each place in succession, ending with Grub N' Go.

"Okay," Gomez said and turned to Dwayne. "This is where you come in. Why was there a body in your freezer?"

In rapid succession, Dwayne looked from Gomez to Shelly to me to Moody to the door leading to the front, then to the door leading to the back to the floor to the ceiling back to Gomez and finally to Shelly. He cleared his throat and brought his hands together in front of him. This was what a caged rat looked like.

Moody stood, grunted, opened the freezer door, and walked

in, disappearing in a plume of swirling white vapor.

Dwayne scuffed a foot on the brick floor. "Brian must have done it the other day. We rarely go in that freezer."

"Liar!" Shelly shouted. "Brian would never kill someone. He was with me the entire time."

"Not the entire time," Dwayne said. "Brian came back."

"When?" Gomez asked.

Dwayne looked at me before responding. "Early this morning. Way before we opened."

Gomez narrowed her eyes. "Did he tell you he was coming this morning?

Dwayne nodded. "He did. I relayed the message to Christi and Tommy."

My neck turned red. I hated it when people lied to me. "Were you here?"

"No. I was at home in bed. He used the key I gave him to get in."

"What key?" Gomez asked.

"He gave Brian a key so he could check out his business for possible investment," I said, then regarded Dwayne. "At least, that's what he told me."

Dwayne stood straight. "It's the truth. I trusted him."

Gomez pointed at the body. "Where does she come in?"

Dwayne told her the story of Brian wanting him to hire two lookalikes. "Christi was supposed to have been a body double for Shelly while she aimed the camera."

"Does she have family?" Gomez asked.

"I think she was single. Not from around here. She had this Eastern European accent. Don't know about her living situation. I think she lived off Oak Street. She was a sweet girl." Tears glimmered around Dwayne's eyes.

"So, probably close to here," Gomez said.

He sniffled. "Seems like it. She walked to work."

The gravity of the situation settled in. Dwayne pulled a paper towel out of a wall dispenser and blew his nose.

Shelly tapped her foot and chewed on a fingernail while staring at the ground. "I take back what I said a moment ago."

"Take back what?" I said.

"That he was around me the entire time." She shook her head in frustration. "He was gone this morning when I woke up. We camped at PirateLand these past few weeks. I love my sleep, and he's always an early riser. He'd slip out of the RV before sunrise and watch it from the beach. Sometimes he'd be gone for a few hours."

"Unaccounted time," Gomez said. "Did you have a car he could have left in?"

"No," I said. "They drove around the country in a camper van."

"Did you all ever take an Uber or taxi anywhere?" Gomez asked.

"No," Shelly answered.

"There's a transit stop outside of the PirateLand entrance," I noted. "I pass by there about every day."

Moody emerged from the freezer, leaving the door open. To Gomez, he said, "There's not much in there. Looks like she was wedged between a wall shelf and the door. When Clark popped the door open, it sprung her out."

Gomez and I locked eyes. I bet we were both thinking the same thing.

"However," Moody said, and everyone returned their attention to him. He shifted unsteadily. The grizzled detective wasn't one who enjoyed having the spotlight turned on him.

"However, what?" Gomez asked.

"However." He lifted a gloved hand to reveal a pair of glasses. "I did find these."

Shelly gasped and sank to her knees. "Oh, no! Those are Brian's!"

CHAPTER
SEVENTEEN

We got Shelly to a chair in Dwayne's office. She buried her face in her hands. Moody pushed Dwayne to a corner of the kitchen, where Battles and Dame kept a close eye on him. The restaurateur had a lot of questions to answer. None of the answers seemed favorable.

Gomez had me comfort Shelly while she went and grilled Dwayne. This was the part where, as much as it pained me, the police took over and kept me out of the loop.

I pulled up a chair beside Shelly and put my arm around her, patted her knee, and whispered nonsense like, "There, there. It'll be okay. It's probably nothing." We both knew it probably was something. Like Dwayne, or someone associated with Dwayne, murdered Christi and did something with Brian.

On that thought, I said something that might uplift her in this dark moment. Or so I thought. "It's not his body out there. We just found his glasses, but not him."

That made things worse. Shelly's sobs turned into a wailing cry.

I kept my mouth shut.

I wished I could be a fly on the kitchen wall while Gomez and Moody questioned Dwayne. I wasn't sure if they would keep me in the loop or not. Gomez always said she wasn't supposed to tell me anything about murder investigations, although she did on a few occasions. That was her first case, she later told me, and she just wanted to get it solved. Maybe after they interviewed Shelly, she would relay what was asked and what they told her.

A few hours later, after taking Dwayne into custody and getting statements about our travels this afternoon, Gomez sent us home. I took Shelly to the Wal-Mart in Surfside Beach near my house so she could pick up some clothes and toiletries. We went back to my house for the night. After changing the sheets, I gave her my bed and slept on a sofa in my office on the other side of the house.

I'm not sure how much she dozed. I slept like a log and woke up with a crick in my neck.

* * *

The next morning, I took her to breakfast at Johnny D's Waffles in Surfside. She didn't want to talk much as we sipped coffee at a table in the corner, waiting for my parents to arrive. We were both numb from our shared experience last night. My parents came in while we were browsing the menu. I invited them with Shelly's permission. They lived around the corner and drove their golf cart to get here.

Gomez put out an APB on Brian, but on this busy Memorial Day Weekend, with so many tourists and campers in town, the police already had their work cut out for them as it was. While Brian's camper van was nice, it blended in with the many others coming and staying at Lakewood, PirateLand, Ocean Lakes, and the other campgrounds in the area.

Shelly had nothing to do but wait. She had called her parents and Brian's parents this morning and gave them the news. All were going to catch a flight from Louisiana and head this way. There might not be any available until Tuesday.

The events of yesterday afternoon happened so fast that by the time it was over, all that had transpired was difficult to take stock of. Brian abandoned Shelly, then traveled to the various restaurants where he'd had combative situations with the owners to apologize. Why do that if he was going to leave Shelly? Didn't he know she could have found him at one of those places?

From everything she told me about Brian, he seemed like a smarter-than-average fella.

Then, finding the body of Christi in the freezer escalated the situation. I might have thought her death and Brian's disappearance were two separate things had Moody not discovered Brian's glasses in the freezer. Shelly said he was as blind as a bat without them. That there was no way he would have the vision to drive anywhere without them. Then where did he go? Who killed Christi? Brian, Dwayne, or some other heretofore unknown figure? Was something else happening that we weren't aware of? Something bigger?

She checked her phone every few minutes. Still hadn't heard a peep from Brian. Her thin hands gripped the phone like a vise.

I poured myself a second cup. "He'll turn up"

"I hope he's alive." She bit her bottom lip.

"Me too."

At that moment, I found myself angry with Brian. How could someone leave such a pretty and sweet girl all alone thousands of miles from home like he did? It made me want to find him and at least give him a good talking-to. I wasn't one for violence, but this situation brought those protective urges to the forefront.

My parents sat down across from Shelly and me and exchanged greetings.

"This is my mom, Nancy, and dad, Lloyd," I told Shelly.

"Pleased to meet you," she said. Shelly had picked up a pair of denim shorts and a teal Coastal Carolina t-shirt at the store last night. She hadn't heard of the school before coming to Myrtle Beach, but she liked the color and the cartoon chanticleer on the front. It made her look like a local and not a tourist.

My dad rarely comes with a filter. He looked at Shelly and me, laughed, and said, "This looks like it could be Parents Week at Coastal, and she's showing you around while you're in town."

Mom snickered. Shelly guffawed. My face turned red. Had to give him credit. He got me there.

A server came, took our orders, and departed.

Mom and Shelly chatted while dad listened. I sank into my world. Autumn and I used to go out to breakfast early on Sunday mornings. Johnny D's opened after she passed away, but I bet she would have loved this place. They had great, in-house-made breakfast hash. She would have gotten that with an over-easy egg on top and let the yolk soak into the potatoes and corned beef.

I looked up from my reverie as a server set an ooey-gooey red velvet waffle down in front of me before placing a Cinnaroll waffle in front of Shelly.

Twenty blissful minutes later, we left Johnny D's. No doubt a few pounds heavier, but it was oh-so-worth-it after the night Shelly and I had. She told me she was feeling sick to her stomach from the nervousness. The sweetness and cinnamon of the waffle didn't help.

Mom offered for Shelly to go back with them to their house

and spend the day. Mom said she'd take care of her. Shelly agreed and hopped on the back of their golf cart and puttered away.

I drove north on Kings Highway out of Surfside and into Myrtle Beach toward the Boardwalk and my bookstore before veering left onto Ocean Boulevard. A few low clouds drifted out over the ocean. Sunlight glimmered off the waves. The fronds of the palmettos were still. Seagulls cruised about with ease. I stopped several times on my way to the store to allow tourists dressed in beach clothes to cross the street to the beach.

I arrived at the bookstore and unlocked the door, flipped on the lights, and then punched in a code on the beeping security alarm console to disarm it. Shelves of books in the front and rear of the store stood silent from their nightly vigil. The sense of solemnity I got every time I came here early in the day hadn't dwindled since the day Autumn and I first opened the store. The store was tranquil during this time.

I let out a breath and smiled. That might have been the first time I'd done that since yesterday. Besides the waffles, there had been little to smile about today. I glanced at my home away from home: the coffee bar. Knowing what was to come calmed me and pushed the thoughts of last night away.

I checked the clock. Winona would be here in about half an hour at 11:30 to assist me. Margaret was coming after church and lunch, and not a minute before. Sunday afternoons aren't busy. Once Margaret came, I could leave.

I readied the coffee bar. Winona let herself in, said hello, and went about getting the cash register ready. Five minutes before the store opened, I sent Gomez a text, asking her if she'd learned anything about Brian's whereabouts. I didn't expect her to get back to me, but it was worth a shot.

When the noon hour came, Winona walked to the front, reached up on tippy toes to flip the Open/Closed sign, and unlocked the door. As soon as she did, a man entered. I stood behind the coffee counter. Winona greeted him, which he ignored. He craned his neck, looked in my direction, didn't like what he saw, and kept looking elsewhere.

"Help you?" I called across the store.

He stopped in his tracks. When he stopped moving, I recognized him. It was the mystery man from Grub N' Go last night. Curtis.

CHAPTER
EIGHTEEN

Curtis froze in his tracks. He wore an expensive navy sport coat, khakis, and white shoes. Modern business casual. For the day, I wore flip-flops, golf shorts, and a t-shirt proclaiming my left-handedness and for righties to give me some elbow room.

He said. "I'm looking for someone, and I heard she may be here."

"Who are you speaking of?"

"A young woman named Shelly." He held a hand out even with his right shoulder. "Stands about yay tall. Pretty girl. You're Clark, right?"

"Guilty as charged. She would have been here, but she's not feeling well."

"Where is she now?"

"With my parents."

"Oh, okay. Besides not feeling well, how is she?"

"Shaken. Confused. Stomach tied up in knots." Although she did a banger job scarfing down the sweet waffles at Johnny D's.

He had a deep Cajun accent. Made me miss New Orleans. He sounded like an educated Foghorn Leghorn.

I said, "We saw you last night and chased after you. It about got me arrested."

"Why would that be?"

"Boardwalk patrol thought I was chasing her," I said. "They tackled me and dragged me to an alley for questioning. She came back a few minutes later and vouched for me. Otherwise, I might have spent the night in jail."

"Sorry to hear that," Curtis said. "I didn't see you. When was this?"

"We saw you walk out of Grub N' Go. She chased after you, but you got lost in the crowd."

"Believe me," he said, "I wanted to find her and Brian. I didn't see you or her last night. After leaving Dwayne's place, I walked around the corner to where I parked my rental and went back to the hotel."

"Do you know what happened to him?"

His head turned in a short arc. "No. I'm here to find him, but I heard they found his glasses in the freezer at Grub N' Go along with the body of some girl."

"How'd you hear that?"

"I have sources."

His flat gaze left no doubt that he did. I admitted, "I was the one who discovered the body."

He closed his eyes for a long second. "I'm sorry you had that happen to you."

"Not the first time," I said.

He canted his head to the side and brought his eyebrows together as the door chimed as two tourists walked in. Curtis approached where I was at the coffee bar, so we weren't speaking to each other across the store. Winona stepped out from behind the counter on the other side and went to help, or distract, the new customers. That girl was sharp, which was why I picked her to manage the second Myrtle Beach Reads location.

"Coffee?" I asked Curtis as he bellied up to the bar.

"None for me. Thanks," he said.

"How did you know where to find Shelly?" I asked.

"Brian's daddy."

"When did you last speak to his dad?"

"He called me this morning."

I asked. "What were you doing at Grub N' Go last night?"

"Same thing I'm doing this morning," he said. "Looking for Brian. His daddy is worried sick about 'em."

"Why?"

"They haven't spoken to each other in about six months," Curtis said. "While they were chasing BBQ places out in the Badlands of South Dakota, Brian stopped returning his daddy's calls and texts. He knew Brian was out doing his own thing before taking over the business and thought little of it at first. Mr. McConnell knew they set Myrtle Beach as their last stop, so he sent me here. He's worried about his boy. As a parent myself, I feel for what his momma and daddy are going through. Not to mention what's supposed to happen when Brian gets back."

"You mean taking over the family business?" I asked.

He blinked at me. "Where do you come into the picture?"

I made a brief introduction and explained how Shelly and I met.

Curtis closed his eyes and shook his head from side to side. "Oh, that poor dear. I'm sorry he did that."

"No need to apologize to me," I said. "Do you think it's because of what he was getting ready to transition to?"

His shoulders dipped. "Dunno. Could be. He saw what the job did to his daddy."

I looked at Curtis. "That's what I don't understand. If your business has a board of directors in place, why put the load on one person's shoulders?"

"Good question," Curtis said. "His daddy always wanted input or final say into everything that went on with the company. We don't deal with the overall vision of the chain, just making sure that what he directs gets done."

"I'll be the first to admit that I don't know how big businesses like yours conducts themselves," I said, "but it would seem to me that if Brian's dad needed to step back, that he would allow the burden of certain aspects be handled by you all instead of everything falling on Brian's shoulders."

Curtis bobbed his chin up and down. "Oh, believe me. That's what we, as a board, discussed outside of his daddy's presence, but it's not our call to make."

"Could you make it your call?"

There seemed to be an easy back-and-forth to our conversation. Until this point. His next words, although delivered in his Cajun easy-going way, sent a shiver down my spine.

He said, "We could if Brian never returns."

CHAPTER
NINETEEN

We exchanged contact information in case either of us learned anything about Brian's whereabouts. Curtis left with a cup of coffee and a Lee Child book tucked under his arm.

I called Mom and had her tell Shelly that I spoke to Curtis. Shelly's only response was that his being in Myrtle Beach made sense now that she thought about it. Being twenty-four hours after Brian abandoned her, she was going to go call the police and file an official missing-persons report after she got off the phone with me. The police had already sent an alert out to bring Brian into custody on sight, but Shelly wanted to make it official on her end. Mom had made her a grilled cheese and sweet tea for lunch. She said her stomach was doing better and that she and my dad were debating which type of berry pie was the best since dad loved dessert and Shelly grew up on a berry farm.

I hung up the phone and tried to go about my business, but I couldn't focus. I worked behind the coffee counter. The day was slower than I would have expected for the Sunday before Memorial Day. Everyone must be on the beach. I couldn't blame them. It was a beautiful day outside. I set myself on descaling one of my Bunn commercial coffee machines. I used it to brew whole pots of coffee on the counter against the wall. A gleaming silver Astra commercial specialty coffee brewer sat on the other side of the counter for cappuccinos, lattes, etc. Erin Howard bought it for me after solving her father's murder.

As I labored, I started thinking. Yesterday, Shelly and I had visited all the places where Brian might have gone that she knew about. Now, with the police on the lookout for him, there was nothing much for her or me to do. We had to play the waiting game. So, that's what I did.

I replayed last night's events in my head over and over, trying to figure out what Brian's plan was. If he had a plan, that is. It's possible the pressure on him mounted to where he became unhinged. It started with getting into arguments and progressed to possibly killing a seemingly innocent victim. What was his next move? Was he still in Myrtle Beach? Did he know the police were after him? What was his endgame?

My back was to the store as these thoughts and questions danced in my head in a continuous loop when a soft, lilting voice said behind me, "Excuse me. Do you serve tea?"

I turned to answer and saw a woman of average height standing on the other side of the coffee bar. That was all that was average about her. She had blonde hair pulled up into a loose bun. Two curly locks of hair floated down over a freckled face. Her skin had been kissed by the sun. She wore smart, black-framed glasses, giving her an attractive librarian kind of vibe. I couldn't see much from the neck down but based on the six words she said to me and my first sight of her, I'd hire her on the spot.

My heart thumped. As my mind raced, I realized I needed to answer her. "Uh, yes. I do. From the Charleston Tea Plantation."

The skin around her nose crinkled for a moment. It was a cute crinkle. "I'm not familiar with it. Do they have an Earl Grey?"

"They do."

"Great. Thanks. Can I have a cup?" she asked, then looked over her shoulder where a little girl wearing a cornflower blue dress played on the train table in the kid's section, laughing gleefully. The woman smiled as she turned back to me.

"Coming right up. Yours?" I asked, tilting my head in the girl's direction.

An ear-to-ear I-can't-help-but-smile smile appeared. "Yes. Libby."

"She's a cutie," I said and meant it.

"Thanks." The woman fingered an earring dangling from an earlobe. "She's a special little girl."

I almost said, as would have been characteristic of me, "That's what all parents say," but for some reason, I didn't. Instead, I said, "She looks it."

"Thanks. Libby's been through a lot," the woman said in a somber tone. She glanced at my left hand, bit the corner of her mouth, and stuck a petite left hand over the counter. "Andrea Crispin."

I reached up and shook her hand. There was no ring on it. I figured that's what she was checking on mine. The hand was cool to the touch. "Clark Thomas. Nice to meet you. You all on vacation?"

"No. We just moved here."

"I hear that a lot. Where from?"

"Missouri."

"Missouri? People move here from up north, not from the west. What brings you out here to the South Carolina Coast?"

"Business."

"Oh, what kind of business are you in?"

"Furniture and home decoration sales."

I stared at her with what had to be a dumbfounded look. She noticed and filled in the blanks. Pointing over her shoulder, she said, "I bought the furniture store next door."

"You mean Coastal Décor?"

She laughed. It was a cute laugh. "Is there another furniture store next door?"

It was my turn to chuckle. That was something I would say. "I didn't know Sherry was selling."

"Well, she was ready to retire. Libby and I needed a," she hesitated a beat, "a change. So, I took my savings, put in an offer, and voilà, here we are."

My chin bobbed up and down while maintaining eye contact. I couldn't look away and neither could she. "Yes, here we are."

A few seconds passed. I didn't know what to say. I felt like I was supposed to be doing something but forgot what.

"So, tea?" she said.

I stood up straight. "Yes. Let me get that started for you."

"Great. Besides the Starbucks at the Barnes and Noble in Market Common, it's hard to find good, hot tea around here."

"That's a good spot," I said. "Do you live in Market Common?"

She twisted her lip. "Yes. In Paradise Hideaway. Know of it?"

"I think. Is it the salmon-colored building near Tidal Creek Brewery?"

"That's it. It's cozy. Great neighborhood to walk in."

I could speak to this woman all afternoon. There was an easiness in our conversation that I hadn't experienced since–

"Mommy! Mommy!" the little girl yelled as she rushed across the store to Andrea. We broke eye contact.

"What is it, Junebug?"

While Libby told her mom about a book she found, I set about heating water for her tea.

"It'll be a few minutes while the water heats up," I said. "Go ahead."

She followed Libby. I couldn't help but watch her go. She wore a simple white blouse and a skirt decorated with flowers that fell below her knees, showing she had curves in all the right places in a subtle way. The little girl took Andrea to a shelf and pulled out a Mo Willems Piggy & Elephant book.

Andrea directed Libby to take it to an empty table in front of the coffee bar.

"I love these books!" Libby said as she came within earshot. "I haven't seen this one before."

"That's great, Libby," Andrea said. "Have a seat and look at it. I'll be right back."

"Okay, Mommy," the little girl said and cracked open the book that had big, bright illustrations.

Andrea left her there and came back to the counter. "Sorry."

"No need to apologize," I said. "Anything for her?"

"I know it's blazing hot outside, but do you have a hot cocoa you can make for her? Small."

"Coming right up," I said.

Her smile was intoxicating. I almost couldn't look away but forced myself to, determined to make the best hot chocolate that I'd ever made in my life for Libby. The hot water for Andrea's tea had finished heating. I grabbed a cup and set it on the counter, along with a packet containing her preferred tea bag. I laid a lid upside down beside it.

"Here you go. If you need cream, honey, or sugar," I pointed, "they're down by the end of the bar. Give me a minute on Libby's cocoa, and I'll bring it to ya."

Andrea wrapped a delicate hand around the cup. "Thanks. What do I owe you?"

"Nothing."

"Nothing? Come on. I don't accept charity."

"Think of it as a welcome gift."

"Okay." She bit her lip again. "Thank you."

I leaned forward and tilted my head in a conspiratorial manner. "Besides, if you're going to be next door, and you like this tea, I'm sure you'll be back."

She placed her left hand on top of the counter and gave the wood a stroke. "I'm sure I will."

CHAPTER
TWENTY

Later, after Andrea and Libby — sadly — left the bookstore, I told Winona that I was leaving. Mom was making dinner. Margaret had arrived to start her shift.

I hadn't spoken to Shelly since earlier and still had no word about Brian. The wait was getting to me. I couldn't sit still or stop fidgeting. I figured an evening with Mom, Dad, and Shelly could help. I realized being with friends might help as well. The problem was, I didn't have many. I'd call Chris, but he and Erin were cavorting on some island in the lower Caribbean. After that, my choices were limited. I considered reaching out to Gomez, but she probably had plans with her boyfriend or was on a case. The boyfriend, whoever he was, wouldn't approve.

After I drove past PirateLand where Brian and Shelly had stayed during their time in Myrtle Beach, I came to the Neighborhood Wal-Mart stoplight where the Lakewood Camping Resort was and pulled to a stop at the front of the pack.

To my right was a Murphy Express gas station. That's where I normally got my gas. As I looked up to check the current price of fuel, I noticed a camper van pulling away from one pump and making a left toward me and the stoplight. It looked like the same van that Shelly and Brian drove, but it was without the 2 Foodie

Nomads markings.

As it came closer, the driver looked left in my direction. He was clean-shaven and without glasses. He wore some sort of thick, black glossy hat. Despite his appearance, the eyes gave him away.

It was Brian.

He swung the RV right to head south on Kings Highway and gunned it. The campervan accelerated with a velocity I didn't think possible for a vehicle of that size.

My light was still red. I looked both ways. A family in an overloaded golf cart was puttering from the campground across the intersection as my light turned green. Once they passed, I pushed the Jeep's accelerator to the floor.

The chase was on.

* * *

The thing with attempting a high-speed chase through Surfside Beach and into Garden City was the multitude of stoplights. On an ordinary day, a person could spend tens of minutes sitting at one of the eleven stoplights in the seven miles between 544 in Surfside and the split of 17 into the Murrells Inlet MarshWalk.

This was no ordinary day. The odds were with Brian. We zoomed through the green light at Platt Boulevard and again at 5th Avenue North in Surfside Beach. He got over into the left lane as he sped through the light splitting Surfside Drive and Glenns Bay Road. I had to wait for a Range Rover to inch by before I could join him there. Only one vehicle separated us. I clutched the steering wheel in a vice-like grip. Blood roared through my ears.

I don't know if I blinked for the first two miles. My focus was on his van and side-view mirror to see if he was looking back at me. We made eye contact once or twice, but I wasn't sure if he knew who I was. Not a single cop car was in sight.

The man drove like a maniac. He changed lanes five or six times, weaving in and out, as we sped past Tupelo Bay. We were in the right lane as we clipped by Greg's Cabana. Brian saw an opening in the left lane and swerved into it. The entire camper van wobbled on unsteady wheels with the sudden move. A sudden move like that in my Jeep could cause it to flip over. It surprised me that his RV didn't.

I looked in my side-view mirror. A line of cars with no break was coming up on my left. There was no getting over behind Brian. I stepped on the gas and caught up with him. We raced alongside each other. I blew my horn. He jerked his head to look over at me for an instant before returning his attention to the road.

Then, his vehicle veered away from me. He merged into the turn lane, going to Atlantic Avenue. I had no choice but to keep going.

Several of the cars that had blocked my access to the left lane followed Brian into the turn lane. I couldn't get over in time and passed through the intersection.

I looked back to see Brian swing left onto Atlantic and swing around a golf cart headed toward the beach and away from me.

Two thick rows of idling vehicles were at the light to go in the opposite direction. I merged left into the center lane in front of McDonald's. Good fortune was with me again as two drivers stopped to give me room to turn into the fast-food parking lot. They presumably thought I was on a Big Mac run. They would be wrong.

I zoomed around the line of cars waiting at the drive-thru and exited the rear of that area that emptied out into Kroger's parking lot. A narrow road flowed behind the Tsunami Surf Shop and Wings Beachwear shopping center. I took it back toward Atlantic and Brian. Two big trucks waited behind two golf carts to pull onto the avenue.

Brian's RV was nowhere in sight. He must have already passed by Angela's Fresh Market stand to my right. An empty field covered with grass divided the street I was on and Angela's.

I drove a Jeep for a reason. Jerking the wheel to the right, the big tires bumped over the curb and into the grassy field. I made a beeline for Atlantic. No one was coming. I barreled across the lot, throwing up plumes of sand and grass, and thumped back onto the two-lane road, heading for Brian.

I passed by trailer parks on both sides of the road. The Village Surf Shoppe separated them on the left side of the road. His tall RV was visible in the distance. An area of marshland separated the mainland from Garden City Beach. A causeway bridge spanned the watery area. The right side of the crossing had a walkway. Several fishermen leaned against the railing, with lines cast into the water.

Brian was passing by Sarah J's when he cut into the oncoming lane to get by a slow-moving golf cart. He veered rapidly back into our lane to avoid an oncoming minivan as it came off the causeway bridge, only to get behind a puttering golf cart. The causeway bridge was coming up fast. He jerked the wheel left so hard that the entire driver's side of the campervan was visible.

The move was too much for the RV. It went up on two wheels and tipped over with a crash. The speed with which Brian was moving had enough momentum to cause the RV to roll side over side toward the bridge. I was powerless to do anything.

Traffic and time stopped. The fishermen dropped their poles and dove out of the way.

Brian's RV rolled with such speed and angle that it hit the side of the bridge and soared several feet into the air. It tumbled over the edge and into the marsh below landing with a thunderous crash.

A white truck raised up in front with a lift sped past me to the bridge. Several vehicles were between me and Brian. None of them were moving. Everyone stared in horror at the scene. An eerie silence followed.

I stopped the Jeep in the middle of the road, jumped out, and ran toward the causeway. Time slowed while my heart raced.

The white truck with the funky lift stopped near where Brian went over. Three men hopped out. One of them seemed to struggle as his friend had to support him. All three went over the side to help Brian.

I was almost there but couldn't see what was happening.

People had climbed from their cars and stood, watching the scene. One woman close to the RV shouted, "They're trying to help! Please save him!"

A moment later, the three men reemerged from the side and, without speaking or looking at anyone, climbed back into their truck, hit the throttle, and zoomed across the bridge to the other side of the causeway and the Garden City Peninsula.

Sirens wailed in the distance. Help was on its way.

I arrived at the bridge huffing and puffing. Debris from the wreckage was strewn across the road. The camper van had landed on its side in the marsh. It was already half-buried in the pluff mud. Crabs scurried through the muck.

The three men's appearance and sudden disappearance bothered me. Why do what they did?

Then I found the answer through the driver's side window.

Brian was crumpled to his side, his neck bent at an unnatural angle.

But you know how most car chases end in movies, with—

The RV exploded, throwing flames, smoke, plastic, glass, metal—in all directions—and me with it.

The concussive force of the blast threw me ten feet backward off the bridge and onto the Atlantic Avenue pavement. I landed against the side of a Honda coupe, denting it. Then darkness.

CHAPTER
TWENTY-ONE

Total darkness. I lay on my back on a hard surface. My chest felt like Godzilla was standing on it. Then my entire body jolted. I opened my eyes for a second and saw a blue sky with plumes of rising black smoke above me and two people. One on my left. One on my right.

"Hang in there," one of them, a woman, said in a calm voice.

My eyes closed again. They were closed for a long time.

* * *

Time was a flat circle and meant nothing. I regained consciousness at a slow pace. The sense of feeling came back first. I wished it hadn't. I HURT. All over. Smell came next. Antiseptic. Then hearing. Beeps and muffled voices.

My eyes opened. An angel with dark hair stood above me on one side. Her scruffy poodle was on the other. Not a poodle. Detective Moody.

If he stood on one side, then the angel must have been, "Gomez," I croaked through dry lips.

She grasped my hand. An IV line was attached to the back of it, covered with gauze. An area of it was red with blood. My blood.

I almost fainted, but held on. My ears rang with an intensity that muffled the volume of . . . everything.

Moody stepped aside and Dad appeared in his place.

"It's okay, Clark," he said and took my other hand for a second before letting go. "You're going to be okay."

Gomez held her grip, for which I was thankful. Her hand was soft. Comforting. Just what I needed.

"Where's Mom?" I said at length.

"At home waiting for Shelly," Dad said.

"What?" I asked and pointed at my ears. "I'm having trouble hearing."

"Your eardrums ruptured," he said louder, "from the explosion."

"Oh, that."

I didn't realize it at the time, but Dad later told me I was yelling during this entire conversation, so they all projected their voices as well. It seemed like my normal voice, and theirs.

The events that occurred before I blacked out came rushing back to me. Brian. The camper van. A chase down Kings Highway through Surfside and Garden City. A crash and explosion on the causeway bridge. Pain and darkness. The next thing I knew, I was here.

They waited for me to gather my words and thoughts. There was no rush.

I looked at Gomez. "Brian?"

She shook her head from side to side and took a deep breath. "He didn't make it."

"Has anyone told Shelly?"

"Not that I'm aware of," Dad said. "An Uber picked her up a while ago to take her to Target to get a few things."

"Did she forget something?" I asked. "I took her to Wal-Mart to get a few things last night."

"I don't know," Dad said. "She's been gone a couple of hours."

"We haven't reached her either," Gomez said.

I groaned, partly in pain, partly because of her vanishing and the questions it raised.

Gomez squeezed my hand and released it. It was a sad moment. "Take it easy. Moody went to get your doctor and nurses. They're going to take care of you. Then we'll talk."

"How long has it been since it happened?" I asked.

Gomez looked up at a clock on the wall. "Four hours."

"How long before the crash did Shelly leave?" I asked Dad.

He scratched his head. "I'm not sure. A while."

The simple mental math needed to figure out how long she had been gone wasn't working in my head. I didn't need to know the exact amount of time. She'd been missing for far too long. It didn't take over four hours to go to Target and back. I instructed Dad, "Call Mom. Check on Shelly."

"I'll do that," he said and left the room.

At once, a tragic thought struck me. I tried to sit up, but Gomez placed a hand on my shoulder to hold me in place.

"Stay there," she instructed. Normally, she spoke with authority. A person used to being in charge. When she told me to remain in place, her tone was different. Caring. Compassionate. I couldn't help it, but feelings of affection stirred.

Moody returned and said the doctor was on her way.

I said, "A white truck was there. One of those monstrosities with a Carolina squat." I had to catch my breath. I was having difficulty breathing. The doctor would tell me to keep my yapper shut once she came in, so I needed to get my immediate recollections out now. Gomez held up a cup of water and a straw for me to drink from. When she pulled it away, I said, "Thanks. Does anyone know what happened to that truck?"

Gomez looked across the room at her partner with a questioning look and then turned to me. "What did this truck do?"

"It pulled past everyone up to the bridge. These three guys climbed out and jumped over the bridge to help."

"Wow, that's gutsy, heroic, and foolhardy all at the same time," Dad remarked.

"It is," Gomez agreed. "Then what happened?"

"Uh, they came scampering back to their truck, climbed in, and sped away."

"Did they say anything to anyone?"

"Not that I recall."

"That's odd. How old would you say these men were?"

"I don't know. Early twenties maybe. Late teens. It all happened so fast." I wrinkled my brow. "It was weird."

"What was weird?" she asked.

I shifted on the bed and groaned. Pain shot up through my back. After I lay back and took a few deep, cleansing breaths, I said, "It seemed like two of the guys were carrying the other guy between them. Like they were helping him."

"You're right. That is weird," Gomez said.

"He didn't seem well."

Gomez glanced at her partner. Moody grunted.

"Okay." She bit the inside of her right cheek, then looked at her partner. "Put out an APB."

"Will do," Moody said and stomped out of the room.

After he left, I asked Gomez, "Was there anyone else in the RV?"

She moved back and ran a hand through her dark hair. "Um, not that I'm aware of."

"Has anyone checked?"

"They're having to wait to go over the camper because it needs to cool off. They were getting ready to go in last I heard." She paused. "Do you have her number?"

A heavy feeling settled in my stomach. "I don't. Didn't have the occasion to need it yesterday. She was with me the entire time. When I needed to speak to her earlier, I called Mom. Shouldn't you have already had it from when she called the police yesterday to report that Brian was missing?"

"I checked on that," she answered. "We have no record of her calling."

CHAPTER
TWENTY-TWO

I was genuinely confused. The pain in my head wasn't helping. "What do you mean, you have no record of her calling? The first time I saw her, she was screaming into her phone at some 911 dispatcher."

"I don't know what to tell you. I checked," Gomez said. "We had no calls from her. I cross-checked the number she gave to Officer Dame last night on the Boardwalk, and we had no record of that number calling. If she had called, we would have gotten her name and the number would have shown on the caller ID."

"This makes no sense," I said and noticed for the first time that I was wearing a hospital gown. Good thing I was lying on my back with Gomez here.

"I'm going down to my car to get my laptop. I'll pull up Dame's report and call the number." She gave my hand a quick squeeze and left.

I wondered what her boyfriend would think of that. Then it occurred to me I didn't care. I was grateful she was here.

Autumn would have brought a sleeping bag and a suitcase. They would have had to force her to leave my side had she been alive. I missed her so much at that moment. The hole in my life gaped wide.

* * *

The prognosis from the doctor was two broken ribs, bruised lungs, a concussion, perforated tympanic membranes — or busted eardrums in layman's terms — and multiple stitches needed to sew gashes caused by flying glass and shrapnel.

The doctor advised that I stay overnight for observation, but I wasn't having that. It would be difficult to talk or breathe for a few days because of the bruised lungs and broken ribs. The doctor prescribed oxycodone for the pain. It would take my ears a couple of weeks to heal. I hoped people wouldn't mind me shouting. Dad helped me limp out of the hospital later that evening, looking like three B words: beaten, bruised, and bloody.

There was another B word I felt: betrayed.

* * *

Someone returned my Jeep to the house. I spent the night in one of Mom and Dad's guest rooms. The story was all over the news, both local and national. Someone later told me that CNN talked about the explosion and death of the restaurant heir for twenty seconds. They mentioned my name because I had to be taken to the hospital. My phone beeped or rang every few minutes with calls and texts from many people, including Chris, Winona, Karen, Marilyn, Margaret, Humphrey, Theresa from I Heart MB Tees, Gloria and Natasha from OceanScapes; Antonio Bianchi, from my escapade on the Golden Mile, called me from somewhere in the Caribbean. I let most calls go to voicemail and played them back or spoke to a few using speaker mode, holding the phone's speaker against my ear. Even Myrtle Beach's mayor,

Sid Rosen, called, as well as Ed Moore and Morty from Gladiator Games. Ed told me that the police department cut him a check for false arrest during the Connor West case. He laughed all the way to the bank.

Casual acquaintance and news reporter Erica Sullivan wanted an exclusive interview. I declined.

I found sleep difficult. Not only because of the pain but wondering what happened to Shelly. Was she in the RV with Brian? Did she tell Mom that she called an Uber to take her to Target, but someone else picked her up? If so, who? Why? What about the body we found in the freezer at Grub N' Go? Was she related to this? These questions circled my medicated head well into the night.

The blinding flash of the explosion was stuck in my brain. I wondered if I would get post-traumatic stress disorder from the entire event.

Karen called again and said that Humphrey had called out. It was Memorial Day, and I figured he'd been out partying and was too hungover to come in for the morning shift. I was his age once. He also got paid last Friday, so his pockets were full. I remember those last few days before paydays, living off cheap eats like ramen noodles until the money came in.

The store was short-staffed today as it was. Margaret's granddaughter was graduating from high school in Greenville, SC, on Tuesday, so she and her husband were in the Upstate. Winona and I were scheduled to close the store this evening. She had family in town from Minnesota and was going to spend the morning with them. She could open and close the store by herself—one reason I tabbed her to run the second eventual Myrtle Beach Reads location in Garden City—but I would not pull her away from her family. Karen was good at many tasks but opening and closing by herself weren't two of them. She didn't like to be alone in the evenings and early mornings, especially after I found Paige Whitaker's body by the back door. Couldn't blame her there.

That left me. If nothing else, I could go, unlock the doors, and get the coffee going. Then, I could shut myself in the office and put my feet up. My presence in the building was all Karen needed during the morning hours.

Memorial Days weren't typically busy. Most tourists around the Boardwalk spent the day at the beach or walking the promenade. The bookstore was off that beaten path. The only times the store was busy on this particular day was if it rained. That's happened twice since opening the store a decade ago. Precipitation wasn't in the forecast for today.

I informed my parents over a breakfast of eggs, toast, and coffee that I needed to go to the bookstore for a few hours and why. They, of course, didn't like the idea, but relented. They had met Karen. I called her and told her I'd meet her at the store.

So here I was, a man in his early forties being dropped off at work by Dad like a kindergartner being dropped off for his first day of school. It was comforting and weird at the same time.

Karen waited at the front door of the bookstore while I lugged myself up the two steps to the covered walkway of The Shops on the Boardwalk as Dad pulled away. The humidity was palpable already. A stray car and golf cart motored past us on Ocean Boulevard. A trio of seagulls flew by overhead. One squawked at me. The air carried a pungent aroma from the ocean.

She about dropped her pocketbook when she caught sight of me. Her mouth fell open. She rushed forward to help me to the door, grabbing me by the wrist. I told her on the phone that I was going to have a difficult time hearing with the busted eardrums, so she would have to raise her voice if she wanted to communicate with me. She had no problem with that. "Gracious, Clark! You look like you just came out of battle."

"Thanks, Karen. I feel like it." I grimaced as pain shot through my ribcage.

"Are you alright?" she asked. Her eyes were wrought with worry.

"I'll make it," I said. "Let's get inside, and I'll be okay."

I reached into a pocket and handed her the keys. "Here, unlock it for me. It's the key with the book at the top."

The keys jangled as she took them. "Sure, sure."

She unlocked the door and guided me inside. The alarm panel beeped as we entered. I entered the code, and it stopped.

The quiet solitude of the empty store greeted us. I felt better already.

* * *

After getting the coffee going, I had Karen handle the rest of the sequence of opening the store. She said she could handle it and told me to sit down. She thanked me for being here for her and called me a fool for doing it. I didn't argue.

Yes, I owned a house. It's a nice one on a lake a mile from the ocean in Surfside Beach. However, this bookstore/coffee shop is my *home*. It makes me feel at peace. It's where I want to be and where I belong. That sense grew after Autumn's death and the house stopped feeling like home. That had been our place. Her memory echoed in every room. When I was there, I would have memories of her in each room, wherever I was. As long as I owned that house, she would be a part of it. I never wanted to let it go. I treated it like one of those protected historic homes and had changed nothing since that tragic night three years ago.

Since her death, I haven't changed the design of the bookstore either. She did almost all the decorating in it, but when we opened all those years ago, she still had her full-time job at the courthouse. Her appearances here had been few and far between. We'd co-owned the store, but I'd run it. Her commitment, dedication, and that the store didn't earn enough during her lifetime to justify her leaving, kept her in her job.

At ten, Karen unlocked the door. The last of the Myrtle Beach Mystery Blend from Benjamin's bakery dripped to the bottom of the carafe in the Bunn coffee maker. I had also brewed a light roast from Tidal Creek and a dark roast from Birchin Lane Coffee, hitting the trifecta of great coffee from local roasters.

She came back to the coffee bar after opening the door. "No one outside this morning."

I poured her a cup of coffee and set it on the counter with a wince. "Here you go."

It was her morning routine of having a cup of coffee to start the day, so I knew to have it ready.

"Thanks, boss," she said, wrapping her fingers around the handle.

"What did I tell you about calling me that?"

"Calling you what?"

"Boss."

She cradled the mug in her hands and smiled. "I don't know what you're talking about, boss."

I wobbled my head. "Go on. Get your half-and-half and ten

sugars or whatever you put in there and get to work."

She dropped her head. "I'm gonna. You go sit down somewhere. I got this."

"Thanks, Karen."

She stepped over to the end of the counter and prepared her cup from the accoutrements. I slid from behind the counter with a cup of coffee in both hands to keep my torso upright and made it back to my office. I didn't feel like sitting in the boxy gray seat in the corner of the office, nor did I want to sit up straighter in the chair behind my desk. Instead, I unplugged the laptop and took it to a set of recliners set up at the side of the store by a window facing the side street and the hotel next door. It didn't have the best of views, but it was a comfortable chair. It sat near the literary fiction section.

I eased into the seat. Pain shot up my legs and back. I could only imagine how severe that would've been, had I not been on the pain meds.

Before opening the laptop, I sipped the coffee. It was earthy and smooth. Then I sent Gomez a message asking if she had learned anything about the body in the freezer or Shelly's whereabouts. I didn't know what she would, or could, tell me.

The laptop never opened. My eyes closed, and I fell asleep in that chair. I dreamed that Gina Gomez and I were on the date we never finished at the Chapin Art Museum last year. It almost ended with a kiss, our lips almost meeting, but a tiny hand on my knee prevented it, awakening me.

I opened my eyes and looked into those of an angel. A little angel.

CHAPTER
TWENTY-THREE

The hands were soft and small. She placed one on either knee.

Her mouth moved, but I couldn't make out what she was saying in my groggy state.

I blinked a few times to clear away the cobwebs of sleep. Goodbye Gina Gomez. If almost anyone else would have woken me up, I would have been cranky. Not this time.

I managed a smile. It must have looked sinister, with all the scratches and bandages on my face and neck, but she didn't seem to notice.

"Hi, Mister," she repeated. I read her lips and thought she said, "My mom needs help."

The little girl had bright blue eyes and kinky curly blonde hair tied back in a bushy ponytail. With freckles across her cheeks and a big smile, the little girl had an endearing quality that made me like her immediately.

"Oh, hey," I said after clearing my throat from sleep. I pointed at one of my bruised ears. "Speak up a little. I can't hear too well right now."

Her nose and forehead wrinkled. In a louder voice that I could just make out, she said, "Jeez, mister. You look like you've been in a fight."

"Not quite."

"And lost," she continued.

I tried to smile. It hurt. The pain meds must have worn off. The rest of me hurt as well.

"Libby, right?" I asked.

"That's right," the little girl responded as her mom—speaking of visions of angels—stepped around the corner of a bookshelf filled with travel guides.

"Libby," she called and came up short when she saw me in the chair. "Oh, dear. What happened to you?" I read her lips, trying not to be distracted by them.

I pointed at my ear.

"Speak up, Mommy," Libby said. "He said he can't hear too well."

I heard that. "Yeah, I have two ruptured eardrums."

She took in my appearance with the scratches and bandages. "Were you at the bottom of a mosh pit at a Metallica concert or something last night?"

"I would have much rather been there. Spent a few hours in the emergency room."

"What on earth happened?" Andrea asked, holding a hand to her chest.

"I got too close to an RV blowing up."

Her eyes had already been wide since she caught sight of me. They widened further. "Was that you? I heard about it on the news. Such a tragedy."

"Yup. That was me."

"What were you doing there?"

"That's a long story."

Andrea looked at a smartwatch on her wrist. "We have time.

I'm intrigued."

"Libby said you needed some help?"

"Yeah, I just wanted some more of that wonderful tea you made me yesterday. My store is closed today, and I'm working through some inventory and needed a break."

"Let me get up, and I'll get you some."

I started to get out of my seat, but Andrea placed a cautioning hand on my shoulder and held me in place. Her touch was gentle and comforting and a total shock to my system.

"Would you mind if I got it? Your coworker has several people she's helping right now, and I didn't want to bother her. Libby must have found you sitting here and figured you could help me."

A jolt of pain shot through my chest as I sat back in the comfy chair. "Yeah, that's fine. Did you see where I got the hot water and tea bag from yesterday?"

"I did."

"Then help yourself. I think I'm gonna sit here for a while."

"You better," she said. To Libby, "Hey hon, go over to the kids' books and pick out a few, come back, and sit on the floor here." She pointed to a spot on the other side of the vacant seat beside me. An empty identical chair sat to my left.

"Yes, Mommy," Libby said, and disappeared around the corner.

Andrea looked down at me. "Can I get you anything?"

"Can you pour me a cup of coffee, please?" I handed her my mug.

"Sure thing. Cream or sugar?"

I held a thumb and forefinger close together. "A dribble of cream if you would please. Just enough to change the color. I'd appreciate it."

"Okay, I'll do that and be right back. You really don't mind if I go behind your counter?"

"Not today."

"What if your coworker sees me back there?"

"Tell her I said it's cool."

Before she left, she reached down and touched my wrist. "I don't know what happened to you, but you should be home in bed."

"I know."

She walked away, and even with my hardness of hearing, heard her mutter, "Stubborn man."

* * *

I closed my eyes for a few minutes while Andrea was gone. The dream with Gomez didn't return. There wasn't time for it.

The aroma of coffee preceded my eyes opening. My sniffer was like a bloodhound for java.

"Here you go," Andrea said.

I sat up in my chair and accepted the proffered steaming mug of coffee. "Thank you."

She dropped into the chair beside me, one leg tucked under the other, with a cup of tea clasped between her hands. She gestured at my coffee. "Did I get it right?"

I looked inside the mug. The color was a little creamier than I preferred, but I wasn't about to make a big deal out of it. "Looks great. Thank you."

Libby had chosen a stack of books and sat on the floor next to Andrea, leafing through them.

"Tell me what happened to you," Andrea said. She tucked a lock of blonde hair behind an ear so she could sip her tea. The vapor of steam wafted up from it.

"Don't you have inventory or something to do? I don't want you to waste your time with me," I said.

She smacked away an imaginary fly. "Pshh. It can wait. You look like a man who needs to let it all out."

I wasn't sure how she could tell that, but after taking a drink of coffee, I told her every detail about my adventures over the last two days that I could remember. Sometimes having a sounding board, this time Andrea, and getting everything out in the open helped me see the bigger picture.

The first thing she said when I finished wasn't about Shelly, Brian, camper vans, explosions, or car chases. It was, "Wait a second. You're a bookstore owner and an author?"

"Something like that."

"Fascinating. Your wife or girlfriend must have a hard time keeping track of your schedule."

I closed my eyes and breathed out. "I don't have either."

Her back straightened. "Oh, I would have thought that a handsome man like you at your age, no offense, would be taken, or are you one of these new girlfriends every week kind of guys?"

I tried to laugh. It hurt. "Not that."

"Then what is it?"

"I was married to a wonderful woman named Autumn, but she passed away about three years ago."

She placed a hand on my wrist. "Oh, bless your heart. I'm so sorry."

"Thank you. It happened fast. One morning, we took a walk on the beach. That evening, I received word that she had died at her desk at work of a heart attack."

She placed a hand on her chest. Tears welled at the corners of her eyes. "I feel so sorry for you."

"Thank you." I had been told similar sentiments in the three years since Autumn's passing. While my responses were always courteous and kind, if not redundant, it always struck a chord deep inside to bring it up.

She said, "You poor dear. With that and what you went through this weekend, you've been through a lot."

I almost told her about solving three murder cases, but this wasn't the time for it. She wanted to learn about what happened over the weekend. Since she would be next door, there would be time to talk about those if they came up. If she wanted to.

Looking into her probing blue eyes, something about her made me want to open up.

But right now, I hurt.

"Listen," I said, "you've been making me do all the talking. I'm a little in pain. Your turn. Tell me about you."

She placed her teacup on a side table between chairs. "There's not much to tell. I'm from southeastern Missouri." She pronounced the state name "Missour-a" with a bit of a southern accent. "Went to college at Mizzou for fine arts. Graduated. Did this or that for a while. Got married. Like you, my husband died suddenly."

"Oh, I hate to hear that. I'm sorry."

"Don't worry about it. He was a drinker. Was out late at a honky-tonk not long after Libby was born. Had too much to drink and tried to drive home. He never made it. Wrapped his truck around a tree."

If the loss saddened her, she didn't express it. Her attitude toward her husband's death was more of "he did it to himself."

I gave a sympathetic smile. "I'm sorry."

"Don't mention it. These things happen."

"That doesn't mean they're okay. Especially with losing a loved one."

Her eyes studied mine. One of hers twitched. This conversation had quickly ventured into the deep part of the pool. Too quick for someone I'd just met yesterday.

Changing the subject, I asked, "Do you sing?"

She cocked her head to the side. "Only in the shower nowadays. Why?"

That brought up a quick mental image that I had to push away and felt guilty for having. "You have this smooth voice with a bit of a crackle to it, like at the end of sentences when you're excited. It just seems like you'd be a good singer."

"Why thank you. I used to sing in a little country band when I was in my twenties in Missouri."

"Did you travel around?"

"Yeah. Just played some small gigs here and there. We had dreams of going to Nashville, but it never played out. Two of my bandmates got corporate jobs. I waited tables. Far less adventurous than my college days."

"That's how it goes for most of us. As we get older and have sown our oats, we stay close to home. You let on like you used to travel in your younger years. Like where?"

"My stepfather was from Venezuela. He's been my dad for as long as I can remember. My real dad left Mom when I was a baby, so I have no memory of him. Anyway, we used to go back to his home in a town named Morichalito."

"What's your favorite thing about that place?"

She placed a finger on her chin and uncurled her legs on the seat. "Two, actually. It was just this bucolic, picturesque place that was so unlike any large town in the US. And the food. Oh my God, the food. It was incredible. His mom made the best *pabellón criollo*. It was to die for."

"What is that?"

She closed her eyes for a moment and pressed her lips together. "Oh, it's this wonderful mixture of rice, plantains, beans. I don't know how to describe it other than it's the best thing I've ever eaten. Have had nothing like it since."

"A shortage of Venezuelan restaurants in Missouri?"

She laughed. "There's a shortage of a lot of things in Missouri. Don't get me wrong, it's a wonderful place. It's just that Libby and I needed a change. That's why we came here. My husband made a good living, and we'd stashed away a good chunk of money. I used it to buy the business next door."

"Change can be good," I said.

"Or bad if your spouse passes away."

The customers having left, there was no one in the bookstore besides Andrea, Libby, Karen, and me. I had finished my coffee. Andrea took the last sip of her tea. The sounds of Turkish soap operas carried across the store from Karen's phone. They were her passion. Her husband fished. She watched those. I never asked how a country girl like her got into them to begin with. Libby flipped the pages in her books and giggled from time to time.

"How long have you lived in Myrtle Beach?" I asked.

She held up two fingers. "Two weeks. It's been a blur getting set up at our place in our condo in Market Common, getting everything straight with the business, and getting Libby settled into preschool."

"Wow. I bet. Tried many of the restaurants around here? They're one thing Myrtle Beach is best known for, you know."

She nodded her head up and down. "A few. We eat in most of the time. Anywhere in particular you have in mind?" She cocked a presumptuous eyebrow.

At least, looking back on it, I figured that part out. In the present with my aches and pains and concussed head, I didn't catch her drift. Had I been clear-headed, I might have figured out her meaning behind the question.

Being the bonehead that I am, however, I whiffed on her question. "Yeah, there are all kinds of family-friendly restaurants around here like Nacho Hippo, River City Cafe, LuLu's, Dino Land Cafe. Have you heard of the Myrtle 30?"

"The Myrtle 30? What's that?"

"They say that when people first move to Myrtle Beach, they put on thirty pounds within the first few months because they go out and try so many of the restaurants."

She sat up straight and patted her midsection and flashed a thousand-gigawatt smile. "Hmm. I wondered why my pants were fitting a little tighter."

If I could have bitten my lower lip, I would have done it.

She looked away out a window, perhaps thinking back to the life she once lived. I know I did, remembering fond times with Autumn.

CHAPTER
TWENTY-FOUR

Andrea left the store a few minutes later, saying she had put off inventorying for as long as she could. She thanked me for the tea. I thanked her for the conversation. Normal conversations with a woman close to my age had been few and far between since Autumn died. My chats with Gomez could start out innocent enough before they moved to dead people. That wasn't what I would consider a 'casual' conversation.

The pain I felt upon Libby waking me up had melted away while talking to Andrea. Now that she was gone, it returned. With a fury. I got to my feet and limped to the coffee counter to get some water and then back to the office where my pain meds were. We approached the noon hour when Margaret was due to arrive and relieve Karen for lunch. Winona would be in half an hour later. Mom and Dad was going to come and pick me up at one. We'd run through somewhere and grab lunch.

Several tourists were in the store, browsing through books. Karen could juggle the coffee bar and book counter by herself. The store wasn't big enough that she could lose sight of either. Shoppers tended to be more patient in bookstores, so if a person had to wait at either of the counters for a few minutes, they rarely complained.

I returned to the recliner. Light streamed through the window. Sleep tried to overtake me again, and Mom, Dad, Karen, and Andrea were all correct in saying that I should have stayed home today. Besides being a comforting presence for Karen instead of her being here all alone, I had done little good. I could have stayed at home and slept all morning. Probably should have.

Andrea's appearance had been a great distraction. Now that she was gone, current events reigned supreme in my head. Had Brian been trying to escape his future? Was this what it was all about? That didn't explain Shelly and her disappearance.

I thought back to the first time I met Shelly. She had been screaming into a phone in a trailer home parking lot to, she claimed, the police about Brian disappearing, but Gomez said they had no record of that call being made. Then who was Shelly shouting at?

As the oxy kicked in and eased the pain, a thought jolted me to sit up straight in my seat: what if she was shouting to no one?

If that was the explanation, then it was possible that Brian's death and her disappearance around the same time might have been a smoke screen. If he died trying to move to another life and avoid the restaurant career awaiting him in Louisiana, what was she running from? She could go back to the family berry farm and move on with her life after a period of mourning. I knew from bitter experience it could take years.

If Brian was truly trying to escape when he ditched Shelly, he wouldn't have stuck around Myrtle Beach. He took the risk of her finding him, which we almost did. It was obvious now that he had an escape plan and that it would take time to carry it out.

The body in the freezer troubled me. How did it connect and

how long had it been there? If his plan was to run, then why bother with the extra scenes? Maybe when they were filming the extra scenes, she heard something she shouldn't have. Shelly said she controlled the money in the bank accounts, but he had access to the cash he'd brought on the trip. He could move around without leaving a paper trail.

More was going on here than I knew. My drug-clouded brain couldn't make the connections, but I felt like I had enough information to figure out what had happened and what Shelly's next move was. However, there was a question that didn't get answered yesterday that might give a clue to Brian's ultimate thought process.

* * *

Dad had a legendary sweet tooth. Shelving lined two walls of their walk-in pantry. One side had dinner and lunch options. The other side held Dad's collection of candies, cookies, and other assorted sweets. They hit up the bakery at Lowe's Foods at least once a week to get apple turnovers and caramel sticky buns. When he was in Vietnam, he had to eat all his meals quickly because he never knew when he'd be called into battle. That training was still ingrained in him, but now, instead of picking up his arms for battle after eating dinner, he picked up a sweet treat almost before the dishes got put away. He flirted with Type-2 diabetes but somehow held it at bay.

With this in mind, I climbed into his Volkswagen SUV after Winona arrived for work.

"You look like a dog that's been dragged through the mud," he said as I fastened my seatbelt with a cringe.

"You don't look so bad yourself," I countered.

"How are you feeling?" Mom said from the back seat as Dad merged in with the traffic on Ocean Boulevard. She sacrificed her comfort so I could ride in the roomier front passenger seat.

The pain medications were still doing their thing, and at the moment, I felt pretty good. "Semi-okay. I'm famished."

"Where do you want to go for lunch?" Dad asked.

Here was the other thing about Dad. Not only did he gain the ability to plow through his meals speedily in Vietnam, but he also developed a love of fish. Fried, baked, broiled, grilled, raw. You name it, he loved it.

I tried to smile and said those three little words he loved to hear. "Fish and cookies."

CHAPTER
TWENTY-FIVE

What should have been a normal trip to North Myrtle Beach got interrupted in the first mile. As Dad drove up Ocean Boulevard and we passed through the open grassy area with the beach volleyball courts and into the Boardwalk proper, I saw something that caused me to ask Dad to pull into the center lane and stop.

"What is it?" he said.

"Are you okay?" Mom asked.

"I'm fine," I said and pointed out the windshield. "It's that truck."

The center lane that ran parallel through the middle of Ocean Boulevard from 9th Avenue North to Mr. Joe White Avenue was where local law enforcement would park to keep would-be criminals contained, or for delivery trucks and Ubers to pick up and let people off.

"What about that truck?" Dad said.

The white Chevy truck had a lift on the front of it, but not the back, giving it a crooked profile. Much like its driver.

"I saw it the other day after Brian's RV went over the causeway," I said.

"The guys you saw jump out and try to help Brian?" Mom asked. "The one they put the APB out on?"

"Yup. There were three of them. They jumped over the side and climbed inside the RV. I assumed they were trying to get Brian out. Then they clambered back over the side, hopped back in their truck, and sped away. The RV exploded a moment later."

Mom turned her head to face me from the front seat. "Do you think they saw something like leaking gasoline in the RV that led them to think it was going to explode?"

"It's possible," I said. "That or they lit a match to a can of gasoline or something. They were scurrying like their tails were set on fire."

Dad asked, "And they said nothing to anyone?"

"Nope," I said, looking out the car window to my left and right. On the left side of the street was Ripley's Marvelous Mirror Maze. On the right? Grub N' Go Eats.

* * *

I climbed from the car and told Dad to circle the block. A family of sunburnt tourists in a rented golf cart stopped, allowing me to plod with the speed of a swift turtle across the northbound lane and onto the sidewalk. I waved a "thank you" at them as they kept going.

The promenade was busy today and smelled like the county fair and funnel cakes. Grub N' Go had a line stretching outside. I wasn't about to wait, shouldering past a couple standing at the door and excusing myself while I jumped in front of them. They didn't protest. I figured my current appearance would be enough to deter questions.

As I got to the counter, Andres manned the register, taking orders from customers. After being plunged into doing it the other night while we were here, he must have gotten a promotion.

I stood off to the side while a family ordered five burritos, trying to make eye contact with Andres. He hit a button on the cash register. It *dinged* and the drawer opened for him to make change. When he looked up after counting out change, he saw me, paled a shade, and said, "You must be here for Dwayne."

Barely able to hear him, I read his lips too. "I am. He around?"

Andres had this deer-caught-in-the-headlights look. His eyes widened and his mouth opened. He glanced over his shoulder at the door behind him leading to the kitchen and Dwayne's office.

"N-no," he said.

I bobbed my chin. "Then you won't mind if I go back there and see for sure?"

Without waiting for an answer, I lifted the part of the counter to allow access and plunged through the door into the backroom.

"Dwayne!" Andres called over my shoulder. "Someone's here to talk to you!"

In the kitchen, three workers were busy prepping various meats and vegetables for the grill out front. They glanced up when I entered and had the same scared look. Having various sutured cuts, bruises, cotton balls stuffed in my ears, and walking with a pronounced struggle had had that effect on people.

"Dwayne!" I shouted toward his office. "Dwayne!"

His office door was shut. It opened to reveal two young men of similar height and features standing next to each other in front of Dwayne's desk. It was them. They had bushy hair sticking out of ball caps that were turned around backward. Earrings in both ears. Raggedy facial hair that still needed a decade of maturing to grow in. Zits. They dressed in shirts two sizes too big. The third guy was nowhere to be seen.

As quickly as the door opened, it shut. A vein in my forehead popped out. If it were possible, steam would have escaped from my ears like a Bugs Bunny cartoon. The odds of these guys being here and on the causeway bridge were astronomical.

I reached the office and pounded on the door. "Open up! I know who you are! You were at the causeway! All I want is to talk to you. I'm not the police and they aren't coming."

Muffled voices came from the interior of the office. After a minute, the door popped open. One of the young men stepped aside to allow me to enter. The guy to my right closed it after I was in the room.

The office was already tight and congested. With four grown men inside, it was downright stuffy. The air was warm. Swearing isn't in my vernacular, but if it was, I would have unleashed a torrent of curses at Dwayne and these young men.

Instead, I composed myself and fixed my attention on Dwayne. "Shouldn't you be in jail?"

"No." He folded his arms across his chest. "They brought me in for questioning but had to release me when my lawyer got involved."

I looked at Tweedle Dee to my right, Tweedle Dum to my left, and then at Dwayne. I knew my voice was already louder than it needed to be because of the ears, but I raised it to a rock concert decibel level. "Explain yourselves."

All three men leaned away from the volume of my voice. I pointed at the cotton balls in my ears. "Sorry. Busted."

Dwayne's bottom lip pooched out. He shook his head from side to side. "Explain what? I don't know what you're talking about."

I laughed, not from humor, but from disdain. This was going

to take a fair amount of lip-reading on my part. I crooked a thumb at Dumb and Dumber. "These guys."

"What about them?" Dwayne said. His voice betrayed nothing.

"They were at the causeway when Brian's RV went over the side and exploded and nearly killed me."

"Um," Cheech said.

Dwayne cut him off with a hand. He said, "I can explain this."

"You'd better," I responded.

"Jules and Vincent here work for me as delivery and catering drivers," Dwayne explained. "After the other night, I told everyone who works here to keep an eye out for Brian. They all saw him and knew what he looked like and what he drove. They were down in Garden City after dropping off burritos to an event at Waterford Oaks when they saw you and Brian speed by."

I looked Jules and Vincent in the eyes to gauge Dwayne's truthfulness. Neither blinked nor fidgeted. "That true?"

"Yessir," both said in unison.

"Just like Dwayne said." I wasn't sure if the speaker was Jules or Vincent. Dwayne didn't specify. I thought of him as Chong from the stoner comedy duo. "I was driving. We saw you zip past us. I hit the gas and tried to follow you. Next thing we know, Brian's camper was rolling over the causeway."

"Yeah," Cheech said. "We pulled up, jumped out, went over the side, and tried to see if we could help Brian."

"What happened when you all got down there to him?"

Cheech said, "I pulled open the door, but his neck dangled at a funny angle. I knew it was broken and he was dead. Vincent was trying to get to the other side when he saw flames coming out of the engine."

"There was oil and stuff everywhere in the muck, and it was only a matter of time before that fire was going to get to the gas tank," Chong said.

"And you had the presence of mind to know you didn't want to be anywhere near there when that happened?" I asked.

Jules and Vincent locked eyes. "Yessir."

"When you climbed back up, why didn't you say anything to warn the people standing around?"

They looked at each other again. "We panicked," Cheech said, "and just wanted to hightail it out of there."

"Knowing other people were in danger?"

They gulped. Perhaps they were fraternal twins. They weren't identical, but they shared the same mannerisms.

"I guess so," Chong admitted.

"You guess so?" I said. "Well guess who was the closest to the RV when it exploded?"

Their mouths hung open. Dwayne laced his fingers in front of him on the desk.

"You?" one of them asked.

"That's right," I said. There was no need to go down the laundry list of injuries I sustained. I was fortunate to be alive.

"I'm sorry, man," Chong said.

"Yeah, me too," Cheech agreed.

"Well, me too. It's fortunate that I was the only one injured in the blast."

"Don't forget Brian," Dwayne said and wiped a tear from his eye.

We were silent for a moment out of respect for Brian. The sound of a knife hitting a cutting board in the kitchen permeated through the door.

"Where's your friend?" I asked, erasing the quiet.

"Friend?" Cheech said.

"Yeah," I said. "There were three of you there. Where's he at?"

They harmonized, "Umm."

Dwayne said, "You mean Louie? He's off today. I sent all three of them down to Garden City that day."

The boys' shoulders relaxed. I wondered why.

"Okay," I said, looking all three men in the eyes in turn. None of them wilted under my glare. "It's just that I saw your truck outside and didn't think it could be a coincidence and wanted to see if I could find you to ask you a few questions."

"No worries," Dwayne said. "If I'd gone through what you did, I'd be curious too."

I nodded. "Thanks fellas."

Dad was waiting for me in the same spot he let me out. I climbed into the car replaying the conversation in my head. There was no way they were telling me the complete truth. Therein lies the question: what were they lying about?

As we pulled away from Grub N' Go, I told mom to call the police and report the truck. My instincts told me that Jules and Vincent would be long gone by the time the officers arrived.

CHAPTER
TWENTY-SIX

Twenty minutes later, Dad parked in front of The Flying Fish Market at Barefoot Landing. I wasn't lying when I got in their car and said I was famished. I was. We could have eaten seafood at any of the two dozen places between here and Myrtle Beach Reads. What those other places didn't have was Bombur's Bakery right beside it. I hoped coming here would enable me to kill two birds with one stone.

We got a table overlooking the Intracoastal Waterway. Mom ate her favorite scallops, while Dad had fresh-caught Cajun-style seared snapper. I had fish and chips. We talked about Shelly and her disappearance, Brian's death, and how I felt. The people at the table next to us got annoyed because we had to talk so loud because of my ruptured eardrums. That was one reason why we asked to sit outside instead of in a crowded restaurant.

After we left, I asked Dad if he wanted to go next door to Bombur's and get a cookie. He said he'd never been, but the aroma of baking cookies was already carrying his sniffer to their front door. When Dad was on a mission, all Mom and I could do was look at each other and shrug.

It was mid-afternoon and hot, keeping many of the tourists either on the beach, in pools, or in their air-conditioned hotel suites. We benefited from not having to wait in a long line at Bombur's to get inside. They had the same specialty cookies from two nights ago, and I already knew I was going to order a White Chocolate Gandalf's Beard cookie. Mom might have a basic chocolate chip cookie. Nothing fancy for her. Dad would likely order one of everything.

The other night when Shelly and I came, we had hoped to speak to Izzy, the owner. Shelly's messages to the bakery owner went unanswered. Instead, we spoke to Jessica. She told us about how Brian became unhinged and nearly got thrown out. It was the same story we heard at the other locations, but with one wrinkle. Brian asked her about a specific scene in The Lord of the Rings. I hoped to talk to her again about it, and Izzy as well if she were available.

Sure enough, both were working behind the counter. Jessica ran the register while Izzy put the orders together. Dad was in heaven. While he and Mom discussed what they were going to order, I kept trying to get Jessica and Izzy's attention. With my present appearance—having looked like I just stepped out of a trauma unit—that wasn't difficult.

When Izzy first caught sight of me, she stopped in her tracks and tugged at the sleeve of Jessica's blouse. Izzy was heavyset and had a thick head of curly hair that grew in all directions. She looked like a hobbit without hairy feet. Despite her appearance, I knew her to be a sharp woman and an excellent mother to two cute children. We met through various business functions with the Chamber of Commerce.

She turned and poked her head through a doorway leading to the kitchen and yelled someone's name. A moment later, a college-aged girl bound through the door and took Izzy's place.

Before leaving the counter, she grabbed a cardboard box made to look like a treasure chest and stuffed a variety of cookies inside. She excused herself from Jessica and the newcomer, pulled off her apron, and came out from behind the counter.

Izzy was larger than life in many ways. She was also loud. In my current state, her normal volume was plenty high for me to hear.

"My goodness, Clark!" she said as she stepped up to me and placed a hand on my wrist. "You look like an orc beat you with the broad side of a curved sword. I saw you on the news."

"Yeah," I said, "I hate it when I'm on there."

"For goodness' sakes, stop doing things that get you in the news."

"I wish. These things have a way of happening to me."

"I know. I've been watching and reading." She stared up at me. "By the way, congratulations on the book. I read it."

"Thanks," I said with a smile. "What did you think of it?"

She held out the hand that wasn't holding the box of cookies flat and wiggled it up and down. "Meh. Wasn't my cup of tea."

I stifled a laugh. My first book had received mixed reviews, but I was determined to take the negative reviews and learn from them to make my next book better. Izzy wasn't the first person to tell me to my face that they didn't like it. I got hot under the collar the first dozen times that happened but turned the negative into a positive. At least they'd read the book.

"It's not for everyone," I said, "but thanks for reading."

Always coming to my defense, Mom said from behind me, "But I liked it."

Dad said nothing. He was staring at the box in Izzy's hand. I swear he licked his lips.

"Who is this?" Izzy asked me.

I did the introductions, and Izzy guided us to an empty table in the corner. The line had backed up out the door again, but Jessica and the young girl working beside her had things handled.

She set the box on the table after we were seated and opened it, and said, "Have a cookie if you'd like."

Dad picked up a Mt. Doom Chocolate Chip Cookie and held it up like it was the One Ring. "Are you sure?"

Izzy nodded. "Of course. It's my place. If I want to give out cookies, I'll give out cookies. Enjoy!"

"Thanks," Dad said and then escaped into the depths of Mordor via chocolate chips. Mom helped herself to a cookie I couldn't identify, but they covered it in candied walnuts. I helped myself to a Mt. Doom myself.

Izzy grabbed a cookie, sat back, took a bite, chewed, and said with her mouth still full, "I can't believe you survived that blast and are here today."

"Me neither," Mom agreed.

Izzy nodded in her direction and then came back to me. "I heard it was that Brian guy who came here the other day to record a review. How did you get mixed up with him?"

I gave her the short version of it. Mom filled in the blanks surrounding the time Shelly disappeared since it happened on her watch.

"That's crazy," Izzy said, then pointed a finger in the air. "*No.* Brian was the one that was crazy. May God rest his soul."

"What happened here to make him go off?" I asked.

"You tell me," Izzy responded. "He got all high and mighty and demanded more free cookies when they were getting ready to leave."

"Had he had free ones before?" I said.

"Sure. That's one of their perks for doing the reviews. We gave them two of every cookie."

I did the mental math in my head. "About a hundred dollars in free food."

"Closer to eighty, but yeah."

"Let me get this straight, he demands free cookies. You all say 'no,' and then he goes ballistic?"

"That sums it up."

"He snapped at a couple other places too," I said. "I know they had to come in here and talk to you before they started shooting their review. How did he seem then?"

Izzy placed a hand on her chin and squinted. "Bored. Disinterested. Looking out the window, like he'd rather be anywhere else than here."

"Was he that way on camera?"

"Oh no. When they hit Record, he was a different man. A character. I mean, they gave a great review of my little bakery."

"But you wouldn't give him any more freebies?"

"No. It was getting toward the end of the night, and it was like it is now." She waved a hand at the shorter-than-normal line outside. "Our supply was dwindling, and I didn't want to run out of cookies."

"Oh," I said.

Dad chomped down on the last of his first cookie and reached for a second. Mom listened to our conversation with interest, nibbling on her cookie like a squirrel with a nut.

Getting to my reason for coming, I said, "Jessica told us he asked about a specific scene in the Lord of the Rings where Frodo tried to leave and continue the journey on his own but Samwise

Gamgee insisted that he come along and nearly drowned in doing so. Were you around for that?"

Izzy nodded. Her big hair bounced. "I was. I mentioned he looked like a man who would have rather been anywhere else than here. I got to thinking about him asking that question and my impression of him."

"What did you conclude?"

Izzy said, "I know they were at the end of this long journey together and that they were getting ready to go home to Arkansas."

"Louisiana," I corrected.

"Right, Louisiana. Anyway, he and that pretty blonde seemed happy together. They held hands throughout. She was focused on the task at hand, but he wasn't. After I saw that news story last night about you and him going on a high-speed chase and then him dying at the end, my first instinct was that he was trying to run but didn't make it."

Her words struck like a mace to the side of the head. Did he die trying to escape from me? If I hadn't seen him at that stoplight, would he still be alive? The thought almost made me sick to my stomach. I dropped the cookie on the table.

Dad looked at the partially eaten cookie like he was going to lay claim to it.

Then another thought struck. How did he know who I was?

Izzy wasn't done. "When he was here, he said something out loud that I think he meant to keep to himself."

My guilty thoughts died away. "What's that?"

"That he wondered what would have happened to Frodo had Sam not joined him."

At the point when Brian and Shelly were here, Brian had

already put the wheels of his plan into motion but knew it was going to be dangerous. The elements of his plot that might endanger Shelly were about to take place. In the end, Brian died trying to escape to another life.

I realized that he might have escaped had he not seen me at the light in front of the Wal-Mart and his life would have been spared. The feeling tied my stomach in knots. Could be the fish/cookie combo.

Shelly disappeared around the same time as Brian's death. The two events had to be connected, and the connections were forming in my head. If I was right, then I'd been a part of a devious scheme. If I was wrong, then I'd look like a fool.

Like the proverb goes — better a fool than a knave, and knaves ultimately wound up in prison for their deeds.

CHAPTER
TWENTY-SEVEN

Dad dropped me off at home after going back to their place and collecting my overnight bag. Mom begged me to stay another night, but I needed to think, rest, and heal. Knowing myself, the latter two would have to fight with my brain to get done.

Mom gave me a bag of Epsom salts that I poured into the bathtub and ran hot water over. She advised that doing that would help ease the pain and promote healing. I never questioned Dr. Mom.

While the water ran, I poured a glass of sparkling grape juice and pretended it was wine. After a few taps on my phone, a playlist of John Allen Howard movie soundtracks played. I eased myself into the tub, sat back, and closed my eyes. The hot water and steam were already helping.

As I sipped the drink, the crash of Christi hitting the floor in the kitchen at Grub N' Go sounded in my ears. My mind ventured back over the past couple of days. With Brian dead, what happened to Shelly? It was possible she went off the grid and caught a Greyhound bus back to Louisiana. Sometimes the easiest explanation is the correct answer. Yes, we'd spent a few days together, but I was still a stranger to her. We all had people like that who we would meet on vacation and get to know over the course of a stay and never see again after that.

What did she have to do with this? Dwayne had hired two lookalikes of Shelly and Brian for the video to stand in for some shots. Was this a style they used elsewhere?

There was another player here who came mysteriously and just as mysteriously disappeared: Curtis. He said Brian's dad had sent Curtis to Myrtle Beach to look for his son. When Brian died, did Curtis up and leave town as well? Job done?

The main song to the movie *The Duelist* played from a Bluetooth speaker on the wall. It was John Allen Howard's best work. The saddening tones of violins brought me back to a key scene from that movie. In it, the hero's girlfriend had just been murdered by the Sheriff of Jackson, Mississippi during a shootout. He blamed himself for her death and lay in a tub full of tepid water while drinking whiskey straight from the bottle. Tears flowed from his eyes. He put a gun to his head and placed a finger on the trigger. He squeezed his eyes shut hard—like I did now, minus the gun—and thought about his girlfriend and how she would want him to go on and seek vengeance for her death.

He opened his eyes wide, released the trigger, and vowed to do that. The actor won an Academy Award for that movie. John Allen Howard won at the same ceremony for Best Musical Score.

Why was I still thinking about this? Brian was dead. Shelly was missing. They had arrested Dwayne Clayton for Christi's murder, although he claimed Brian did it. It's always convenient to blame a dead man for someone else's murder.

Here I was, beaten and bruised. Like the actor from *The Duelist* and feeling sorry for myself. What about Brian and Christi? Vengeance wasn't needed for their deaths, but with Shelly's disappearance, I felt like there had to be more to the story.

I finished the glass, got out of the tub, dried off, reapplied the bandages and wraps, and walked to my office with a towel wrapped around me after stopping in the kitchen for another round of pain meds. The house was dark. The hum of the HVAC turning on broke the silence. This house had often been silent since Autumn's death. I listened to music but watched little TV.

I know the doctor said not to mix alcohol with the medications, but I made myself an old fashioned anyway. The sparkling grape juice wasn't doing the trick. After doing that, I went into my home office and sank into an easy chair near my desk. A wrap around my ribs further constricted my breathing. The music of John Allen Howard followed me.

I reached for the laptop on my desk and pulled it to me. The power cord got tangled halfway, and it was a pain, and painful, to uncoil it from a leg of the desk.

I went to Brian and Shelly's 2 Foodie Nomads YouTube Channel and found their associated social media profiles. I clicked the first link, and the web browser went to Facebook. Her picture and a header image of her and Brian standing in front of their camper van were displayed on the screen. It showed her hometown as Ethel, Louisiana, and a graduate of Louisiana State University in Baton Rouge. She must set her account to "private" because that was all the information Facebook allowed me to see on her profile.

Except for one other morsel. That she was engaged to Brian McConnell. I clicked on his name. His profile had stricter privacy settings. It showed his name, but that was it. Being the heir of a restaurant empire would have me keeping all my stuff private, too. My publisher forced me to create a profile because they said that their authors must have a presence on social media. I hated it with a passion and had Winona run my page. I didn't even know the password. She had logged me in on my computer and never logged out. That was the only reason I could see their profiles.

On each of their profiles, there was a button to send a message. No one had marked Brian as dead yet, so on a whim, I clicked the button. A little white box popped up at the bottom of the screen to the right. A gray dot appeared where his profile picture would have been. Below that was his name. Beneath that, the box read, "Brian lives in Nowhere."

The hometown forced me to smile. If I traveled the country like he and Shelly did, I might list that as my home as well.

The cursor blinked at the bottom of the message box, awaiting my input. I typed "Sup?" and hit Enter. My message appeared in the message box. After a moment, a gray check mark appeared beside it, letting me know my message went through.

I hit the Back button on the browser and returned to Shelly's profile page. The conversation box with Brian remained on the bottom left of the screen. I hit the Message button on her profile, and an identical box appeared beside Brian's. I typed a message asking if she was okay and hit Send. The gray check mark appeared beside it.

I didn't expect her to answer, but you never know. Crazier things have happened, particularly to me.

I left Facebook in one tab and opened another one. I silenced John Allen Howard on my phone. I went back to Brian and Shelly's YouTube Channel. The pain meds were doing their thing. The aching faded into the background, but the old eyelids were getting heavy. Shelly had uploaded all the videos from their tour of Myrtle Beach, except for the last stop at The Trestle Restaurant in Conway. She'd been busy since then, I surmised.

As I watched the videos, starting with their first one at 1229 Shine in Market Common, I observed Brian. He was gregarious and animated in his reviews. He was also very good at them. His insight into the industry gave him a certain air of authority when talking about how the restaurants were run and the taste of the food. He was like a PBS version of Food Network's Guy Fieri. Even had blonde hair, except that Brian's was natural and Fieri's was bleached. Brian lacked Fieri's tattoos and piercings.

Outside, day turned into night. The videos were each about half an hour long, so they took time to view as I searched for clues. Brian had a knack of explaining what the chefs did right and wrong with dishes in a way that never insulted the restaurant owner, somehow coming across as humorous. It was easy to understand how he and Shelly gained a strong following. She was the eye candy. He was the entertainment.

Shelly said little in any of the videos, but she offered well-balanced takes on the food and drinks. She raved about Shine's Bang-Bang Grouper. I've had it several times, and I concurred.

Then the craziest thing happened. As one video ended, I heard a *bloop bloop* sound come from the computer accompanied by the flash of a little black speaker at the top of the internet tab with Facebook. It wasn't the typical *pop* you heard when someone sends you a message. It's the *bloop-bloop* you hear when a person has seen a message in an open chat and their little profile bubble moves down to the line of the latest message seen.

My breath caught in the back of my throat as I switched tabs.

In the little message box at the bottom of the screen that held my message to Shelly, her profile bubble had moved and set off the *bloop-bloop* sound. She'd seen my message!

I moved my mouth, licked my lips, and swallowed. A car passed by the house on the street. An owl hooted from high above in a loblolly pine out the window.

As I placed my fingers on the keyboard to type a message to her, an even crazier thing happened.

The computer *bloop-blooped* and Brian's profile image in the chat box next to Shelly's moved down too.

CHAPTER
TWENTY-EIGHT

I typed the same message to both Shelly and Brian: **Are you OK?**

This time, the bubbles didn't move.

I stared at the keyboard. It was difficult to focus, but I did my best. The meds and what I'd gone through in the past twenty-four hours were catching up to me. I yawned. A lump caught in my throat. My fingers poised on the keyboard, ready to type out a response.

Did Shelly have access to Brian's Facebook profile? If she handled their social media accounts, then it was possible. Maybe she was riding on a Greyhound bus to Louisiana or something in the dark, moving through farmland, and her phone lit up when I sent the first message. If she was logged into Brian's account, could she have also gotten my message to him?

I wasn't familiar enough with Facebook to know if it were possible to be logged into two Facebook accounts at the same time, so I called my older brother, Bo. He had worked in Silicon Valley for a decade before relocating south to San Diego. He was three hours behind us, and the sun should be going down over the Pacific Ocean.

The phone rang three times before he answered with a laugh. "Sup, Chump? Mom told me you almost got killed."

My brother and I don't speak often. We were both busy men and single. Him by choice, and me by, well, you know. He was four years older than me and a bachelor for life. He played the field like Mickey Mantle. He was a programmer by trade and got in early with Uber, made a ton of money, sold out, and retired to a home near the Torrey Pines Golf Course in La Jolla. Now, he played golf during the day and went clubbing at night.

We couldn't have been more different, but at least we got along when around each other.

"Yeah. Living on the edge like always," I said.

"Whatever, Bookworm."

I smiled. He had called me that since Autumn and I opened the store. In return, I had a name for him. "If you say so, Computer Geek."

We were both in our forties but still ribbed each other like we were ten.

He laughed. Then in a serious voice said, "It must be near midnight where you are. Something wrong with Mom and Dad?"

In the rare times we spoke, the conversation often touched on their health, especially after Mom came down with throat cancer twice.

"Nope, they're fine. Took care of me last night."

"What happened?"

I gave him the Reader's Digest condensed version of everything, leading up to the Facebook messages to Shelly and Brian.

"That's crazy man. Almost makes me wish I could have been there. *Almost.*"

"Yeah, I wouldn't wish what happened on anyone."

"Sounds like it must have been such a rush."

Bo was an adrenaline junky. He climbed mountains, jumped out of planes, bungee jumped from bridges, raced ATVs out in the desert, and went whitewater rafting in the Rockies. If the activity called for a helmet, more than likely Bo had done it.

"Trust me," I said, "It's not a rush anyone should experience."

"I hear ya." He stopped. "Look, I know you wouldn't call me unless you needed something. What can I do for you?"

One could say the same about him, but now was not the time.

I asked, "Can a person be logged into two different Facebook accounts on their phone at the same time?"

He thought about it for a moment, then said, "Sure, it's possible. Kinda clunky, but it can be done. You say this Shelly girl saw your message and then a moment later, must have checked Brian's Messenger?"

"That's what I'm thinking."

"I mean, she could, but I don't know why. You tell me. Did Autumn have a Facebook account?"

My brain stopped.

"She did," I said in a soft voice, drawing out the *did*. "Facebook and social media weren't on my radar when she was alive. After I found the threatening messages on her phone, it got stolen."

"Yeah. You told me about that."

"Here's the thing. I never once thought about her social media accounts."

"You idiot."

I rubbed a hand across my face. Ordinarily, I'd retort with something juvenile. This time? "You're right. I am an idiot. Such an idiot."

"Keep saying that. You might get used to it. It fits you well."

In a more comforting voice, Bo said, "Look. My point is, you never thought to check it after she died. You had no reason to. What you gotta ask yourself is, why did this girl check the Facebook account of her dead fiancé?"

* * *

After Bo explained to me the different ways switching between accounts on a phone might be accomplished, he said the other possibility was that she was using a computer. I said she didn't have one. It was destroyed in the RV explosion. Bo said that didn't mean she didn't pick up another one somewhere else after vanishing or hopped on a computer in a hotel business center for guests and logged into his account.

He said he was getting ready to go out for the evening and hit a few clubs and then said he was going to come to Myrtle Beach and show me how to have a good time. I laughed and said, "No thank you." We ended our conversation with a mumbled "love you" from both sides.

I sat back and looked out the dark window. Not a soul moved. Not even a mouse. I loved living on a dead-end street in a small community. It reminded me of growing up in Southern Ohio. This neighborhood had that feel.

I clutched the phone in my hand, pondering my options. The authorities needed to know about my Facebook discovery.

I called Detective Gomez. She picked up after half a ring. "Clark. How are you feeling?"

Soft music played in the background from her end of the call. "Not as painful as I could be, thanks to the meds. Otherwise, I'm hanging in there. I'm not interrupting anything, am I?"

The sounds of splashing water came through the phone speaker. "No, just unwinding after a long weekend with a glass of wine and a warm bath. My boyfriend is working tonight, so I have the place all to myself and have a day off tomorrow."

The word picture she painted stirred something in my chest. It could have been my broken ribs jumbling around, I wasn't sure, but it was a lovely picture.

I tried to shake the image away, couldn't, but being the man that I am, pressed on. "I just did something similar. Except my bath involved Epsom salts and grape juice."

She laughed. It didn't happen often, but when she did, her laugh had a musical quality that lit up a conversation. "I'm sure you needed it more than I did. So, is this a social call, or did you remember something that happened? Something that could help us find Shelly or figure out what happened to that poor girl in the freezer at Grub N' Go."

"Sorry, it's not a social call," I said. Either the old-fashioned or medications influenced the next words out of my mouth like truth serum. Maybe I should've listened to my doctor and not mixed the old-fashioned with the oxy. "If you want me to call you now and then and talk about something that doesn't have to do with dead people, I'd be up for that."

A pause came from the other end. I pictured her savoring a sip of wine. In a friendly voice, she said, "I wouldn't not answer your call in that case."

I didn't expect the result of this call to be us taking another step in our working relationship/friendship. "I might do that sometime."

"Good," she said. "What's on your mind?"

"I had the craziest thing happen a few minutes ago." I told

her about the messages to Shelly and Brian.

Water splashed on the other end. "Hold on, I'm going to put the phone down and get out of the tub."

I almost asked if she needed someone to dry her off, but held my tongue. After a few more splashes and dead air, she returned. "What time was this?"

I checked the timestamps on the conversation and told her.

"Let me write that down. Just a sec. Okay. You sent her a message to see if she was okay, and Facebook notified you that she had seen the message?"

"Yes. She or someone else."

"And the same with Brian?"

"Yes."

"That doesn't make any sense. He's dead."

Something my brother said opened my mind up to another possibility. "Are you sure?"

"What do you mean, am I sure? Of course, I'm sure. You saw him in the RV and go over the side of the bridge on the causeway before it exploded, and I saw the body. Or, what remained of it. Confirmation on dental records is still out, but what was left certainly fit the family's description of him.

"You're right. It doesn't make any sense. Can I ask you a few questions? Ones that I don't know if you can answer or not."

Ten seconds of silence came on the other end before she breathed into the phone speaker. "I don't know if it's the wine, or that you were a part of this, but I don't mind sharing information with you in this case. You might know more about it than we do. Shoot."

"I take you haven't found Shelly?"

"Correct."

"Shelly told me that Dwayne Clayton hired two people that looked like she and Brian. Christi was hired because she bore a resemblance to Shelly. Another guy, Tommy, I think, was the one who looked like Brian. Did you determine a cause of death in Christi?"

A pause. "We did. She was injected with poison."

"That poor girl."

"Yeah. We think it happened right there in the freezer. There were signs of a struggle."

"Who do you think did it?"

"We checked the surveillance videos, but there was a gap in the recording."

"Let me guess, around the time you think she was murdered?"

"Bingo."

"When do you think that was?"

"Early Saturday morning. Apparently, Dwayne turned off the cameras in the restaurant the night before, but there's a camera in the alley hanging off the side of the arcade that caught Dwayne, Brian, Christi, Tommy, and two delivery drivers, Vincent and Jules."

"I figured they were part of this," I said, and I explained how I tracked them down inside Grub N' Go after seeing their truck parked in the center lane on Ocean Boulevard in front of the restaurant. "They and Dwayne were in there talking about something important, at least it seemed, when I came in."

"We got your mom's call and tried to track them down, but they skipped town."

"Go figure," I said.

"Don't worry. A truck like that will be easy to spot."

"They all look the same to me."

"Me too," she admitted, "but highway patrol is trained to pick out subtle differences in vehicles. Their plate number and a picture of the truck has been distributed statewide and in southeastern North Carolina."

"They could be holed up at someone's house and parked the truck in a garage."

"If that's the case, then they'll be difficult to find."

"You saw them going in," I said. "What about coming out?"

"Here's where it gets tricky. Vincent backed his big truck down the alley, blocking the camera. We could only see the cab of the truck. The rig shook a few times before Vincent and Jules hopped in and drove off. There's a black cover over the truck bed, so other camera angles don't give us an idea of what, or who, was back there."

"When did Dwayne, Brian, Christi, and Tommy emerge?"

"Christi and Tommy never did that we could tell. Dwayne and Brian did. Both looked shaken. We couldn't tell that they said anything to each other. Just nodded and shuffled away."

"You think that was when Christi was killed?"

"We do."

"Tommy too?"

"Don't know for sure, but that was the last time we saw him."

"What do you think happened?"

Gomez let out a breath. "We think the meeting was prearranged, and Dwayne and Brian had planned to kill Christi and Tommy during it."

"Jules and Vincent?"

"Accomplices at the least. Murderers at the most."

"Did you show this video to Dwayne?"

"We did. Picked him up again on suspicion of murder this evening when we put out warrants on Jules and Vincent. He said it was all Brian's idea and that he killed both Christi and Tommy by himself."

"It could be he said that to deflect blame from himself and the two other guys."

"Very well could be. We'll ask those two what happened when we find them. Nothing like blaming a dead person for murder."

"Was there a third flunky around at any point?"

"A third guy? Not that we're aware of."

"There were three guys on the causeway bridge, remember?"

"Of course," she said defensively. "We don't know who the third guy was. Hasn't been a trace of him. It's like he appeared and disappeared out of thin air."

"Were you able to get their phone records?"

"We were. Brian called Dwayne on Saturday evening."

"What time?"

"A shade after nine."

I thought back to that crazy night. "That would have been around the time that Shelly and I were en route to Grub N' Go from Bombur's Bakehouse in North Myrtle. We'd been on his tail up till then, and that might have been his next stop."

"Like he was calling ahead to warn Dwayne."

"Correct," I said. "That also might have been at the same time Curtis appeared."

"Do you think he's involved in all of this?"

"He could be, but I don't know how. This might be one of those rare times that a coincidence in a mystery may be just that—a coincidence." I paused. "Let me ask you this. When those two goofballs backed their truck down the alley, and you saw the entire rig shake, could they have been putting a body in the back?"

"That's our belief."

"Let's say it was Tommy's body that caused the truck to shake. Why kill both of them, leave Christi in the freezer, and dump him in the back of their truck?"

"We're not sure," she admitted. "We asked that question to Dwayne, but he professed ignorance."

"Of course." I gulped and took a moment before continuing. "I think there's something much bigger going on here than we're aware of, and I'm the patsy."

CHAPTER
TWENTY-NINE

Gomez told me she had to get off the phone and make a few calls. I reflected on our conversation after one more happy mental image of her in the bathtub. Six people entered Grub N' Go on Saturday morning, according to the camera, but only four left. Christi was in the freezer. The only way to explain Tommy's missing body was that he wound up in the back of Jules and Vincent's truck. Did they take him somewhere else and dump him? If so, why? If not, then what in the world were they doing driving around with a body for a day and a half?

It seemed like Brian had orchestrated some grand plan, only to have it end with his death. Even the best-laid plans often go awry, as the saying goes.

He was dead. Dwayne was in jail. Tweedle Dee and Tweedle Dum were on the lam. Shelly was nowhere to be found.

After all that happened, a stray phrase Shelly said during our travels shot into my conscience.

I powered the computer on, did a quick Google search, and found what I hoped was the answer to it all.

* * *

I called Gomez back. When she answered, I asked, "Did you mention you're off work tomorrow?"

"Yeah. Maybe. If I can get someone else to check out this Tommy person you mentioned and see if they can track Shelly's movements. We can find her if she is online. We're locked in a holding pattern, if not. Otherwise, I should be free. Why?"

"There's a trip south of here I would like for us to make, but I need you to drive."

"Hmm. You're not in any condition to be behind a wheel."

"The doctor said not to drive for a week."

"Would this be a platonic trip?"

"Completely platonic."

"Is it important?"

"Extremely. I need to get away from here, if only for a day. There's something I want to show you, and I think you'll be very interested."

Ever since I met Gina Gomez, I had known her to be honest and trustworthy. My asking her this question without explanation might reveal if she harbored the same sentiment toward me.

Without hesitation, she asked, "What time do you want me to pick you up?"

* * *

After one of the best nights of sleep in my life, thanks to the meds and rye whiskey in the old fashioned, Gomez picked me up in her Toyota Camry at twelve o'clock sharp the next day. She was dressed in a yellow tank top and a pair of blue jean shorts. Her hair was down and bunched over her shoulders.

She'd said she wanted to keep our trip platonic, but I didn't know how it was going to happen with the way she looked today. I wondered what her co-workers would think of seeing her dressed and looking like this. I know what I thought of it, but I couldn't say it out loud.

I carefully climbed in, said hello, and gave her the address for our destination. She punched it into her nav unit. Within minutes, we were navigating through the warrens of Deerfield.

"Here you go," she said, handing me a printout with a list of names. "What you asked for."

"Thanks," I said, skimming over the list as she backed out of the driveway.

I ran my forefinger down the list as she navigated the maze that is the Deerfield subdivision to get to Platt Boulevard. By the time we turned right onto Kings Highway, I laughed and said, "That's diabolical."

She turned to me, arcing a perfectly sculpted eyebrow. "What is?"

The car came to a stop at the cramped Cheesesteak Factory parking lot in Surfside Beach to pick up subs before we hit the road.

I held up the list and pointed at one entry. "That."

She normally kept it in a tight ponytail. Today, her hair fell over her shoulders. It had a shiny luster and flowery scent of freshly washed hair. It bounced as she shook her head from side to side. "I don't understand."

"Come on," I said, dropping the list on her dashboard and popping open the car door. "I'll tell you while we wait for our food."

* * *

As she pulled back on Business 17, she held the steering wheel with half a hand, unwrapped her sub, and turned to me, "Okay, Clark, run this through for me again."

"It started on Saturday afternoon," I said, while removing the wrapper from the top half of my pizza sub. They loaded it with pepperoni and cheese. Just the way the twenty-year-old in me loved it and the forty-something-old in me might later regret it. I laid out the chain of events that began with me finding Shelly alone and screaming into her cell phone. That happened two days ago, but it felt like an eternity.

I took a bite of my pizza sub, and before it was swallowed, I said, "So, I meet her. She's crying. She's bawling. Doesn't know what to do."

"Right," Gomez said, "because they are a couple thousand miles from home, and she's this country bumpkin."

"Or at least that's how she wanted to come off." After taking another bite, I continued, "She tells me this story of how they are food bloggers traveling the country for a year, doing reviews of restaurants in various parts of the country. She grew up on a berry farm. Brian was the son of some restaurant magnate and was set to take over the business upon his return to Baton Rouge. His dad set them up on this trip as his way of letting Brian do something he wanted to do before devoting himself to the family business."

"And Myrtle Beach was their last stop."

"Yes. But I don't think it was supposed to be their last stop."

"How so?"

"Let me come back to that." I held up a finger. "She tells me that in the past few days, Brian hadn't been himself. He'd gotten into arguments with restaurant owners over what she considered mundane things. She said he hadn't been like that before. That he was the kindest, most thoughtful person there was."

"I wonder if him seeing the reality of what was going to happen caused him to act so erratic."

"I wondered that too for a time."

Gomez flipped her turn signal and moved into the left lane. "When did you think differently?"

"When Shelly disappeared."

"Tell me, Clark, what do you think?" Gomez asked as Business 17 and the 17 Bypass merged in Murrells Inlet.

"That they planned this entire thing."

"Why do that?"

"To make their disappearance plausible."

Despite the traffic flowing at a steady pace, the car braked hard, causing me to jerk forward. Pain in my ribs and back shot up my spinal column. "Oww!"

"I'm sorry," Gomez said. "You said disappearance?"

I rubbed the back of my neck with the hand not holding the sub. It remained intact.

"Yes. Disappearance."

"Why would they disappear? He was due to make a lot of money."

"Money isn't always the most important thing, but Shelly told me that Brian's dad was stepping down because he'd had heart problems attributed to the job. Think about that. His dad wanted Brian to take over the job that almost sent him to his grave at an early age. Would you be eager to do that?"

"My dad was a detective in New Jersey," she said. "Got shot at. Several times and lived to tell about it. Didn't deter me."

"Good point," I said. I didn't have a defense to that, other than, "Some people are different. Maybe Brian grew up in this cushy lifestyle and didn't want to be thrown to the wolves. Maybe he didn't feel that running a restaurant empire was the life for him. Shelly told me that Brian had difficulties telling his dad 'no.'"

"True," Gomez conceded.

"No offense," I said, "but you're one of the toughest people I've ever met. You have this take-no-crap edge to you I admire. Brian didn't come off that way from Shelly's description, nor from the videos I watched."

Gomez ate the last bite of her sub, crumpled the wrapper, and tossed it on the dashboard. "Thank you, I think."

"Don't mention it," I said. "So, she has me run around the Grand Strand trying to track him down, but at every stop, we were always a little late."

"If this is part of a larger scheme, then that's convenient."

"I know. Right? Anyway, the people we spoke to at these four restaurants all painted the same picture of Brian. That he became unhinged and angry when something didn't go his way during their stops. Either the food wasn't good, which Shelly argued wasn't the case, or that one cook was stoned, or they did not give him free cookies. Every time at their last four stops, he made a scene."

"Did this embarrass Shelly?

"That's how I took it. They were engaged, but it showed a new side of him she hadn't seen before and didn't like."

"What was his endgame?"

"Like I said, to disappear. He'd already spent a year dodging his future. Now it was go time, and his back was against the wall."

"How did he orchestrate it?"

"I think he knew all along that Myrtle Beach would be his last stop for two reasons."

"Which were?"

"Dwayne Clayton."

"How does he figure into this?"

"He and Brian were old college buddies. Both come from similar backgrounds. I think Brian enlisted Dwayne to help him vanish."

"Do you think Brian paid him to do this?"

"It's possible. Shelly mentioned he had a trust fund. He probably had money to spare."

"And do what with?"

"I think Brian had been planning this for a long time. Maybe even before he and Shelly ever left Baton Rouge for their tour of the United States. My guess is that Brian paid Dwayne to buy him a new identity but died before he could carry out that plan to the end."

Gomez was silent for a moment as she studied the traffic ahead. "What about the body in the Grub N' Go freezer?"

I tapped on the door handle. The scenario had played out in my head several times. I admitted. "I'm not sure. My guess is that he had planned to stage their deaths and pull a switcheroo with the bodies. Not sure why he would separate Christi and Tommy's bodies before staging their deaths."

The corner of Gomez's mouth inched upward. "Some friend Brian was."

"Tell me about it."

"I get what you're saying about Christi. It's possible. What's the other reason they chose Myrtle Beach?"

I lifted a second finger. "Its proximity to Charleston."

All that was left to see was if my theory was about to play out.

CHAPTER
THIRTY

As we drove forward, it occurred to me that Brian's crazy driving that led to his death may not have been because he saw me sitting at the light. Maybe that was when he was going to carry out his escape plan all along, but he died carrying it out. I just happened to be there when the culmination of his plot began.

The road from Myrtle Beach to Charleston was a straight shot. Miles of pavement lay in between with nary a bend in the road, especially after leaving Georgetown. Route 17 passed through estuaries, marshland, and the Francis Marion National Forest before reaching civilization again north of Mount Pleasant.

Gomez picked up a rock station, 98.1, coming out of Charleston that we listened to most of the way. We would talk about this and that. Nothing important. Casual conversation. It was pleasant. These times with Gomez, er, Gina, as she told me to call her, had been rare. Sparks had passed between us almost from the moment we'd met. Had she been single, it would have been difficult not to ask her out.

She presented herself as a tough person, and in her job that helped. But here, now, talking with her, watching her sing along to old songs from the 90s with a smile on her face, that tough façade melted. Gina seemed at ease with me now, and I was with her. This was a side of her I glimpsed once on the night of the fashion gala at the Chapin Art Museum. I suspected few of her co-workers had seen this side of Gina Gomez.

But invariably, as the Camry sped down the highway, my mind wandered to what happened to Autumn — as I often tended to do. During the miles and miles of forestland and a commercial break on the radio, I asked her, "Ever hear anything about the phone?"

Gina pressed her lips together and looked out the window at the scenery flashing by. "No, not a thing. He said he put it in an evidence bag, wrote some case number that he made up on it, and put it in a processing bin."

"Does anyone else have access to those bins?"

"There's a few, but he's the only one who uses that specific room. He's the tech whiz who can find anything on a computer, tablet, or phone."

"Did you tell anyone else about the phone's existence?"

"I didn't."

"Did he?"

She bit her bottom lip. "I told him not to tell anyone."

"Did he?" I repeated.

"I have no way of knowing for sure, but he swore to me he didn't."

"Do you trust him?"

"Of course. That's why I turned over the phone to him." She took her eyes off the road and faced me. "Look, Clark, this is what I live for. Seeing that people like you get justice for losing their loved ones. I'm the one who told you of my suspicions about Autumn. I did that because my hands are tied."

The car beeped, letting her know she was angling out of her

lane. The computer on board the Camry took over and centered it between the painted lines. She looked away from me and went back to scanning the road ahead. She reached over and grabbed my hand. "Clark, I'll help, and have helped, you in any way that I can."

"I appreciate that," I said and meant it, even though her revealing her suspicions about Autumn's death upheaved my life. Gomez and I shared the same trait, one I didn't know I had until I came across the body of Paige Whitaker. We wanted to see that the bad guys ended up behind bars and that the victims' families had closure. "Some days, it's all that I can think about."

"I understand." She squeezed my hand, not out of love or desire, but of sympathy. Sympathy for me. For Autumn. For what happened that night. "I think about that night, too. With Banner."

Former lead detective, Ed Banner, had called Gomez to come along with him as he investigated Autumn's death. His then partner, Moody, wasn't around, so the up-and-coming Gomez got the call. Banner died a few months later.

"What about it?"

"Just how," she paused, furrowed her brow, and tried to find the words, "just how *off* he seemed that night."

"What do you mean 'off'?"

"Like, he was in charge and didn't let me have any input."

"You said that you were still rising on the staff at that time. He may not have thought you could add anything."

"That's a fair point, but not protocol. When we arrived at the courthouse and found Autumn at her desk, he had me stay outside of her office. Wouldn't let me touch anything, even though I had undergone extensive crime scene training at that point."

"Why?"

"That's what I never figured out."

"Did you get close to her?"

"If you mean, did I examine the body? No, I didn't."

"Did you see anything awry at the scene?"

She drew her shoulders up and expelled a breath. The next words she spoke were done in a deliberate manner. "Not that I could see. Her head was down on her desk. The screen saver on her monitor displayed pictures of you and her." She tsked. "Honestly, it looked like she was taking a nap."

My voice shook. "But she was dead?"

Gomez did a slow nod of her head. She was thinking this through. We both understood the importance of her being able to recall exact details from that evening over two years ago. For the clinical Gomez, her voice took on a sad tone. "Yes, he checked her pulse. There was none."

I tried to play the scene in my head. I had been to her office several times. It was cramped and cluttered, full of filing cabinets, a printer stand, and two guest chairs across from her desk.

"What was on top of her desk?"

"Not much."

I forced a chuckle. "That's Autumn for you. Everything around her could be a mess, but her workstation was always tidy."

"As it was that day. Her head rested on a stack of papers she seemed to be filing away for the day. An uncapped yellow highlighter and a ball-point pen lay off to the side as did a cup of tea."

"That also sounds about right. Autumn loved her tea as much as I love coffee. What were the papers?"

Gomez rubbed a hand across her forehead. "Let's see. It was from a case they heard in court that day."

"Remember which one?"

"I think this one was for a trial that involved the hit-and-run of a seven-year-old girl."

I thought back. "Oh, the Kaminsky girl from Aynor?"

"That's the one."

I remembered watching Nicole Boone and Bob Juback of WBTW report on the story. Abigail Kaminsky had been playing out in her front yard with her younger brother. Their house fronted Elm Street near the IGA. Two men tried to rob Gloria's Hair Supply of hair extensions but didn't know that Gloria packed a 12-gauge behind the counter. The getaway driver went in while the attempted robbery was being committed, and Gloria shot him in the rear end with buckshot as he tried to escape. He and his friend got into their 1990 Honda Civic and escaped the parking lot, but not before Gloria shot out a taillight and the back glass.

While they panicked about what to do, the driver, Lamont, couldn't keep the car on the road and drove right into the Kaminsky's front yard, hitting Abigail while she rode her tricycle. It took months for the case to come to trial, and once it did, the press was all over it.

Autumn said little about it, other than the fallout from the long days would have her working late while the trial lasted. They convicted the two idiots of attempted larceny and second-degree manslaughter. Both are still behind bars with no end of their sentence in sight.

"If Autumn were murdered, it wouldn't have been over that. Those two morons didn't know their butts from a hole in the ground."

"I was around that case. That's true. They were dumb crooks."

We rode without speaking for a few moments. Tom Petty sung about not backing down on the radio. When the song ended, I asked, "Did Banner make or take any phone calls before getting there?"

Gomez rubbed a finger on the steering wheel. "You know what? He did. Twice. Once on the way and then after we left."

"Did you hear what he said?"

"He didn't say much. Mostly listened and said 'uh-huh' a few times."

"Like he was receiving instructions?"

"Could be. Or his wife was giving him instructions about what to pick up for dinner." She turned to me. "Now that we're talking about it, it was these phone calls that originally got my hackles up. I had spent little time around him. He was Moody's partner, but the way he spoke on the phone caused me to think that he was hiding something."

"Any way to find out who he was talking to?"

Her hair bounced as she shook her head. "It was his personal phone. You'd have to get his personal records."

"How would I do that?"

"Don't know that you could or that a call log even exists. You could try his wife. Have you spoken to her?"

"I haven't." The vein on my forehead pulsed. "Could you get me in touch with her?"

Gomez hesitated, considering the question. We were entering a gray area. She wasn't supposed to comment on cases to me, but in this case, there was no case. No official investigation into

Autumn's death existed.

After a moment, she said, "I'll hook you up."

I thanked her and looked out the window as the car drove through Mount Pleasant. Forget Paige Whitaker. Forget Connor West. Forget John Allen Howard. Forget Christi Hunter and Brian McConnell. More than anything in my life, I wanted to find out who killed my wife. What Gomez just gave me was a spark.

When we got back, I'd take that spark and light Myrtle Beach on fire if I had to.

CHAPTER
THIRTY-ONE

We entered Charleston and wove around Ansonborough Square off East Bay Street and parked in the cruise terminal parking area. I enjoyed coming to this historic area of Charleston. The hustle and bustle of the city, the sights and sounds and smells always added a little energy to my step. I needed it today because my step lacked pep and strength. The long car ride caused my injuries to stiffen up. Climbing from the Camry was a painful experience. Good thing Gomez had driven, or I couldn't have made it. We crossed the parking lot and entered a security area.

Gomez had phoned ahead to the cruise line and to the Charleston County Police Department. As she was out of her jurisdiction, Gomez wasn't allowed to make any formal arrests. If I was correct in my logic, then an arrest was about to be made. They sent a bull of a man named Officer Callahan to provide muscle and the authority to make an arrest. We didn't want to be standing guard so near the main entrance in case Shelly recognized us and ran. If she came at all. This could be a wild goose chase, but my hunches were often right.

Callahan wore reflective sunglasses and had biceps as big around as a Christmas ham. After Gomez laid out what we thought would happen, Callahan stood vigil with hand on wrist, keeping watch. He seemed to ignore us.

The Carnival security allowed us to pass their checkpoint and ride across to the boarding area of the ship. The Carnival cruise liner *Sunshine* towered the equivalent of thirteen stories over our heads. From stem to stern, the boat was at least three football fields in length. It was the largest boat I'd ever seen up close.

We stood around the bend which was the last step passengers took before climbing the ramp to board the ship. Outside, buses dropped people off that brought them over from the check-in terminal and immense parking lot. Cruise agents checked boarding passes as they entered the ship.

As we waited for the first tourists to arrive, in a quiet moment, Gomez chuckled and said, "Clark, no wonder you didn't tell me where we were going. I might've thought you were going to sweep me away on a cruise."

A note of real-life seriousness from the smile on her face and the look in her eyes told me that there was a mild sense of disappointment in her words. Would she have accompanied me had we been actually getting ready to board the ship?

The other part of her tone was also that of amusement. I didn't know how to take that. If she and her boyfriend were serious about their relationship, would she jest about going on a romantic cruise with me?

I couldn't speak.

She touched me on the arm. "Sorry, I shouldn't have said that. I have a boyfriend, and he wouldn't appreciate me intimating that I might have enjoyed going on a cruise with you."

"Does he know you're here now?"

She shook her head.

"Is this trip with me something you're trying to keep a secret from him?"

She bit her lip and looked down and to the side. God, she was sexy at that moment. I wished I had two tickets to paradise for us. Forget her boyfriend. Forget the bookstore. Forget the broken ribs and ruptured eardrums.

"I'll take that as a yes," I said.

"Don't tell anyone I'm here with you today."

"Uh, well, if what I think will happen happens, then people will know we're here together."

The entire reason she was here was because of what I told her might happen on this dock today.

She expelled a long breath. "Oh. Right."

We leaned against a railing, watching tourists board the ship. A red-headed woman wearing a Carnival Cruise Line uniform took tickets and greeted travelers. They were departing for a seven-night, five-stop cruise to the Caribbean.

A husband and wife walked past us. She carried a pocketbook over her shoulder. He carried everything else like a pack mule. He towered over her, had a shaved head, and wore a shirt with Grumpy the dwarf on it. She had short dark hair and glasses and clutched her pocketbook strap.

"Poor Brady," she said. "I hope they take good care of him while we're gone."

"Brady?" the husband said in an incredulous tone while he tried to situate a shoulder strap to a carry-on bag over one shoulder. "He's a dog, for goodness' sakes. As long as they give him some food and water, he'll be fine."

They strolled past us as the woman said, "Now, Craig, listen..."

Her voice faded as they climbed the ramp to the ship.

"I think Craig should have kept his mouth shut," Gomez said, forcing me to laugh.

It hurt. "I concur."

She smiled, and we looked down the line of arriving passengers. I had wanted us to arrive early before they allowed anyone to board the ship. The husband and wife with the poor doggy were among the first to arrive.

Then I spotted a familiar face. It wasn't the one we were looking for. I looked away as he and his wife got close, hoping he wouldn't recognize me. Especially in my current state. I'd already drawn a couple of suspicious looks from passengers when they first saw my appearance. I didn't want to talk to this guy wearing a white golf hat, but it seemed like he kept popping up everywhere I went.

He and his redheaded wife walked past us, and I thought I was in the clear. Then he stopped and turned back, causing the people behind him to have to dodge to avoid running into him and his wife.

In a deep, thick Appalachian voice, he said, "Clark? Is that you, buddy?"

I faked a smile. "Hey. Caleb, right?"

He nodded and looked me up and down. "You look like crap."

"Thanks," I said.

Gomez contained her laughter.

"You going to the Caribbean with us?" he said.

"No. Just waiting for someone," I answered.

"Oh, okay," he said with noticeable disappointment.

"We woulda had fun. I stopped by the ABC Store before we

left and stocked up." He held up a red gym bag containing bulky shapes that clinked together.

His wife looked away. She was probably eager to get away, too. Maybe from him.

"I'm sure," I said. "Have a great trip. Bon voyage."

"Yeah, man," he said before climbing the ramp.

"Didn't we see him at the Chapin Art Museum last year during that gala?" Gomez asked.

"Yeah. I think he was drunk then. Looked like he is now."

"Seemed like it. His wife looked embarrassed."

"Wouldn't you be?"

She smiled but didn't answer. We leaned against the railing and returned to watching people board the ship. I had laid out what I thought happened and what was going to happen. When the moment came, it did happen. But I was very, very wrong about what happened. And the body in the freezer now made complete sense.

"There she is," I said.

Shelly was wearing a gray hoodie and sunglasses. She had no baggage and kept looking behind her as she rounded a corner. Gomez and I weren't trying to hide, and in retrospect, we should have.

The country bumpkin from Louisiana had doubtless spent the last two days on the run watching behind her, never once suspecting that someone would be waiting for her when she arrived at the penultimate scene of the crime.

Gomez gasped and I might have as well because walking beside Shelly was a dead man.

At least he was supposed to be dead.

CHAPTER
THIRTY-TWO

He didn't look like Brian, but it was him. Besides cuts to his forehead, his face was smooth and wore no glasses. He donned a black ball cap to cover his curly blonde hair. His first mistake was walking arm in arm with a beauty such as Shelly who wore big sunglasses. By himself, he might have escaped notice. His second was focusing straight ahead instead of on his surroundings. Had I been him, I would have my head on a swivel, noting everyone in my vicinity.

Perhaps it was overconfidence on his part. Ego. Maybe he couldn't see without his glasses. Whatever the reason was, he had conquered the most difficult and dangerous part of his plan, but there was something he couldn't have planned for.

Me.

They strode down the gangway, locked arm in arm. As they were about to walk by us, Gomez stepped into their path. Officer Callahan stepped up beside Gomez and locked Brian and Shelly in an intimidating glare. I limped two steps forward and stood beside Callahan.

They stopped in their tracks. Shelly gulped. Sweat broke out on Brian's forehead.

"Excuse me," Gomez said. "I'm Detective Gina Gomez with

the Myrtle Beach Police Department, and this is Officer Callahan with the Charleston Police Department." She pointed at me. "That's Clark. Shelly, I think you know him."

We couldn't see their eyes because of the sunglasses, but if we could, I bet panic would have been in them, which explained their next move.

They didn't respond to Gomez. They shared a look and ran in the direction from which they came, out the door of the building where buses unloaded passengers under an overhang. A lot of people were making their way to the ship, and we were all fighting against the current. Shelly and Brian used it to their advantage.

They wound through mostly middle-aged and later would-be passengers, causing a calamity. At every chance he got, he would grab people's luggage and throw it behind him. Tourists shouted in alarm. One woman tried to hit him with her oversized pocketbook, but the blow glanced off him. Callahan and Gomez took the lead in the chase, but Brian's gambit forced them to slow down and dodge the flying baggage. I noted the traffic pattern and veered to the right side of the walkway where there seemed to be less movement.

A big white bus entered the drop-off area under an overhang. Brian grabbed Shelly's hand and pulled her in front of the bus, causing the driver to slam on the brakes and honk the horn. The driver didn't see me and moved forward, blocking my view of the two escapees. I ran along the driver's side of the bus as it plodded by. When I reached the end of the bus, Brian and Shelly were gone from view.

I darted outside and saw them cross over Washington Street and into a parking lot leading to East Bay Street. I didn't know what their plan was. If they had a plan.

They had three options. Head left and down toward The Battery and Rainbow Row, go right on East Bay and try to disappear near the Harris Teeter or the aquarium, or go straight through the market and to King Street, where they might melt into the shopping crowd.

Gomez and Callahan caught up with me. I pointed at Brian and Shelly. Callahan said, "Got it," and said something into the radio attached to his shoulder.

"Stay back," Gomez warned me. "Let us handle it!"

I appreciated the protective gesture, and normally I would have ignored her and kept up with the chase despite her admonition. As I've been known to do. Here, as I slowed to let Callahan and Gomez race past—like an NFL tight end and Olympic sprinter, respectively—my body sent a reminder of the state it was in.

My chest heaved and a crushing pain radiated in my ribcage. The other aches and pains came roaring to the front of my conscience, causing me to stop and place a hand on the side of a Truist Bank to catch my ragged breath.

Shelly learned nothing from our night on the Myrtle Beach Boardwalk. Namely that two people running down the sidewalk not dressed in workout gear stood out. Shouts emanated from around the corner, accompanied by muffled *whumps*. Pedestrians on the sidewalk on the opposite side of East Bay stopped and stared at what was happening on my side, but out of my line of sight.

I let go of the building with my legs protesting and limped around the corner.

Callahan straddled Brian, who lay face down on the sidewalk

in front of the bank entrance. Another officer, who must have been on patrol when he got Callahan's call, had Shelly in a similar position. They were applying handcuffs when a cacophony of police sirens blared from nearby.

Callahan looked up at Gomez and gave her the go-ahead nod.

"Brian McConnell and Shelly Garland," Gomez proclaimed, "you are under arrest for the murder of Christi Hunter and in the disappearance of Tommy Toliver."

CHAPTER
THIRTY-THREE

Thirty minutes later, I rested in a chair while sipping on a cup of stale coffee from a Styrofoam cup inside Charleston County Sheriff's Office on Broad Street. I sat across from an information desk inside the front entrance, still trying to catch my breath. My legs ached from trying to run, but the adrenaline rush from catching Brian and Shelly overcame it. Gomez was somewhere in the depths of the station, processing Shelly and Brian for extradition back to Horry County.

My part in this crazy escapade was over. If it came to trial, I'd have to testify, but for now, I wanted to forget about meeting Shelly. Being a good Samaritan got me into trouble again. This time, it almost got me killed. I'd think twice before getting myself into a situation that centered on missing persons or dead bodies.

Maybe.

The door behind the desk opened. Gomez stuck out her head and motioned for me to join her. I struggled to my feet, using the desk to prop myself up as I passed between the gap. Gomez held the door open and gave me a tight smile. I squeezed past through the door, brushing up against her body. Her delicate perfume was intoxicating.

"Sorry," I muttered. It wasn't the most truthful thing to say.

"Don't mention it," she said and closed the door behind her. She held a hand out in front of her. "We're going to the end of the hall. Last door on the left."

We entered a room with wood paneling. A two-way mirror took up most of one wall. We were on the window side. It peeked into a cramped room with a long wood table, four chairs, and a small square window set up high at the center of the opposite wall. It let in a sliver of sunlight that shined on the middle of the table.

Two chairs on one side were empty and rested at awkward angles. Brian and Shelly sat on the other end. They were not talking to each other. They were not looking at each other. Shelly's arms were crossed. Her head was turned away from her fiancé. Brian's hands pressed against the tabletop. The knuckles were white. His jaw was tight. Eyes red. An officer in a blue uniform sat across from them.

A short man and a shorter woman wearing similar rumpled gray suits stood before us. The woman with long dark brown hair looked to be around my age but had a youthful face that could have passed for someone a decade younger. A useful trait to have in undercover operations.

The older man of average height could have been Detective Moody's cousin, with silver banker's hair and bags under his eyes, shook my hand as I entered. In a gruff voice, furthering my suspicion that he was related to Moody, he said, "I'm Hankins. This is Detective Graves. I run the investigative unit here. Detective Gomez tells me you're responsible for the apprehension of these two."

I released his hand and replied, "I didn't apprehend them. Merely pointed Gomez in their direction."

"Semantics," he said. "They wouldn't be sulking in there like crabs caught in a trap if it weren't for you."

"Maybe," I conceded.

"They clammed up," he said. "They will only talk to their lawyer. We've put in a call, but he's in Louisiana. Be a while before he gets here. I heard about his RV exploding on the news. Didn't think that it would spill over down here. You're lucky to be alive, kid."

"Thanks," I said.

"I told Hankins how Shelly came to be on the dock," Gomez said, "but that doesn't explain Brian."

"I know how he did it," I said.

Three other police personnel were in the room. Everyone looked at me for an explanation. I was happy to provide it.

"Hold on," Hankins said and pushed a button below the two-way mirror.

Graves produced a recording device and said the time, date, and everyone present.

Hankins lifted two fingers at me. "Proceed. Start from the beginning."

Brian and Shelly looked at a speaker in the ceiling and then at the mirror. Hankins wanted them to hear my recounting of the events on the off chance that they would screw up and say something they weren't supposed to.

I pointed at a chair facing the mirror. "Mind if I sit?"

"No, please go ahead," Hankins said. "You look like you need to take a load off."

He and Graves stepped aside, allowing me access to a hard plastic chair.

"Thanks," I said again and lowered myself into the chair and faced Brian and Shelly. They couldn't see me, but I could see them, and they were who I wanted to direct my words to.

"This failed plan of theirs nearly ended my life," I said. "I'm delighted to help see they end up behind bars for as long as possible."

Brian scrunched his eyebrows and looked over at Shelly. I couldn't hear her but could read her lips. "Clark."

It wouldn't be difficult for my voice to carry to their room. With the busted eardrums, I still talked at a louder-than-normal volume. I cleared my throat and said, "From what I can tell, Brian might be the kindest, most sincere person on this planet, but he might also very well be a killer. It's an odd juxtaposition, I know, but at this point in his life, he's like a man backed into a corner. On the one side, he has his life. His life with Shelly where he's free to do as he pleased. On the other, he has a business and career that awaited him when he returned home to Louisiana."

I tried to get comfortable and cross one leg over another, but my body didn't allow it. I put my left foot back on the floor and brushed my knees with my hands.

"You know what they say about a man backed into a corner?" I continued. "That they will most likely come out like a wild animal, willing to fight and do whatever they can to escape. I think Brian saw the corporate life and what it did to his dad and went, 'Nah, that's not for me.'"

Hankins and Graves likely hadn't had the time to learn what I was talking about with Brian and this career in Louisiana. They could fill in the blanks later. For now, Brian's face was a mixture of disbelief and consolation. Perhaps he was comforted that someone understood his position.

"Here's what he did," I said. "They are food bloggers who

have traveled around the country for the last year, doing restaurant reviews. This was his way of going on an adventure before committing to the corporate life. He told his dad to give him a year to do something he wanted to do. A big, grand adventure."

Brian nodded.

I said, "I've always wanted to drive across the country, and I'll admit that I'm jealous of him having that freedom. I wish I would have thought about it with my wife when we were their age.

"But that's what it comes down to. Freedom. It's a big, comforting thing in life. Freedom. Knowing you can do whatever you want. Brian is young. I'm guessing in his late twenties. Has most of his life ahead of him. He loves his freedom. It was about to vanish almost overnight.

"So, while he planned this big, long trip with Shelly, with his dad's blessing, Brian was hatching another plan. A magic trick fraught with danger."

"What was the plan, son?" Hankins asked.

"To vanish."

I let the words sink in as I studied Brian. His jaw dropped before he picked it up off the floor.

"I was an innocent bystander at the beginning. Just minding my business, coming home from Marion and passing through Conway when I pulled up to a stoplight and saw Shelly screaming into her phone in a mobile home dealership parking lot. I, being the sucker that I am, pulled into the lot when the light turned green to see if I could help.

"She told me that her fiancé, Brian, had just abandoned her at a nearby coffee shop. She was thousands of miles from home and didn't know what to do. I asked her who she was yelling at on the phone and she said to the police. They wouldn't help her until Brian had been missing for twenty-four hours."

Gomez leaned forward and added, "Shelly never made that call. I confirmed it by checking 911 and dispatch. No one from her phone number called to report a missing person."

"Then who was she yelling at on the phone?" Graves asked.

"The air, I guess," I said. "It was all for show, and I fell into it hook, line, and sinker."

Brian sat up straight in his chair when I said that. She turned to him but said nothing.

"Shelly wanted to get someone's attention so she could tell her story," I said. "For someone like me who offered help, if she said she had already called the police, then I perhaps wouldn't suggest doing it again."

"Did she say why he left her?" Hankins asked.

"She said she didn't know," I answered.

"Ah," Hankins and Graves said at the same time.

"That wasn't the only thing Shelly faked."

"What else did she do?" Gomez asked, her voice etched with irritation. Oops, might have left this next part out earlier. I'd be annoyed at me as well if I were her.

I held up a finger. "Not what she did, but what she didn't do. After we went to Bombur's Bakehouse, she said she was going to text the owner, Izzy, to see if she knew what Brian was up to. We were in the car when she said, and even made the display of texting someone while I was driving, but I spoke with Izzy the day after the explosion. Before we left, I asked her if she got any messages from Shelly the previous night. She said she hadn't."

Shelly stared at a spot on the floor.

"Here's another thing about our dear Shelly," I said. "How

she had to have been in on this. Detective Moody found Brian's glasses in the Grub N' Go freezer. How they got there, I don't know. Maybe they fell off while he was shoving Christi's body in there. His plan was to change his appearance, and when Gomez and I spotted him, he wasn't wearing glasses. Shelly said during our chase that Brian was blind without his glasses. Either he doesn't really need glasses or he's wearing contacts right now."

Gomez pointed a finger at Brian. "Or he got laser eye surgery somewhere along their trek."

"Your point being?" Hankins said.

"The point is," I tipped my head toward the two behind the glass, "if he came back to their RV on Saturday morning without his glasses, wouldn't Shelly have noticed something was wrong?"

Hankins straightened his neck as the other members of the precinct staff nodded their heads in understanding.

"Here is where Brian's dad's plan went awry and the forces of wanting to escape while being an authentically nice guy conflicted." I shifted in my seat. "Over the past year, while they've traveled, he was working with his old college buddy, Dwayne Clayton, to escape. He told Dwayne well in advance when he was coming to Myrtle Beach and to have certain things ready for him."

Gomez held up a finger. "Such as two pawns hired to be body doubles for their videos. Christi Hunter and Tommy Toliver."

I nodded and continued her thought. "New identities. I know from researching while writing my books they can be bought for around thirty-K. Don't forget about hiring goons to help carry out the plan. The younger and stupider the better."

"The question is, why would Dwayne Clayton do this?"

Gomez said. "He's a respectable businessman."

"Yes, he's that, but check into his finances. I bet he was coming up short somewhere. He had to have done this for money. My guess is that he didn't know what he was getting into when Brian first contacted him. Shelly let it slip that Brian came into a trust fund when he turned eighteen. Plenty of money to arrange for new identities and to pay Dwayne and his goons."

"But why go through all that hassle? Spend all that money?" Hankins asked.

Brian and Shelly perked up in the holding room.

I answered, "To make people think they were dead."

CHAPTER
THIRTY-FOUR

"Dead?" Hankins said. "They meant to fake their deaths?"

The police in the room reacted with surprise. Gomez wasn't. I had already told her Brian's motive.

Body language speaks volumes, and Brian's reaction told me I was on the right track. He turned to Shelly and tried to get her to look at him. She stared forward and wouldn't meet his eye. The others on my side of the wall noticed the same behavior.

I said, "Yes. Fake their deaths and escape to an unknown tropical location. It sounds romantic. Doesn't it? Disappearing. To simply walk away. Leave it all behind. The dead-end job. The family you despise. The town or job you feel trapped in. Then the next day, viola, you're someone new. That's what they tried to do. The cruise ship they tried to board here would have sailed for the Bahamas. From there, they could leave the boat and vanish. They would have the entire Caribbean at their disposal."

Hankins crossed his arms. "How was he going to do it?"

"By doing what he did," I said. "Blowing up his van and having people believe he was inside of it."

"Except he didn't get away with it," Hankins said. He grabbed a chair and sat down beside me. Gomez remained standing by the two-way mirror, looking from Brian and Shelly back to me. Graves stood with her hands stuck in her pockets on the other side. Various police officials gathered around.

"Nope," I said.

"Because of you," he said.

"I guess so."

"How did he do it and where did it go wrong?"

I rubbed the top of my thighs. They throbbed. "What went wrong was that he has a conscience and didn't want to see any harm come to Shelly. That's why he left her at that coffee shop. The restaurant in Conway was their last stop. He would have implemented his plan after that. He had been confrontational and acted crazy over the few days leading up to Saturday, but he didn't like people thinking ill of him. Yes, he was about to fake his death, but he couldn't live with these restaurant owners that he rubbed the wrong way to go on thinking that he was a bad guy."

"He was unstable." Hankins said. "Like, he wanted to do this evil thing, but part of him wouldn't let him go out like a bad guy."

"That's the way I see it," I said. "Maybe he's AC/DC or something. Split personality disorder."

"Our psychiatrists will evaluate him," Gomez said. "We'll learn."

"Good luck with that," I said and wondered if his erratic behavior would let him plead insanity and get a reduced charge. I wasn't a lawyer, but that seemed like something he could do. "I'm not sure how much Shelly knew about his plan. The ultimate endgame of faking his death, but she was to be a part of it. When it came down to it, he couldn't bear to put her in danger. So, he changed the plan and left her. The problem was, he had already killed Christi and Tommy."

"When did he do that?" Hankins asked.

"On Saturday morning," Gomez responded. "We have a video showing Brian, Dwayne, Tommy, Christi, and two other men entering his restaurant from an alley beside it. Some time passed before they exited, with the exceptions of Tommy and Christi."

"Brian lured Tommy and Christi there that morning to shoot what they thought was some B-roll footage for their videos," I explained. "Except that they were killed instead."

Hankins waved a hand at the two suspects on the other side of the glass. "So, *they* killed them?"

"I'm not one-hundred percent sure," Gomez answered. "Shelly wasn't at the restaurant that morning that we can tell. I believe Brian set up the scenes where he would shoot from behind Tommy and Christi and would have them eating or something. Then someone would come up behind them and inject them with a needle. We found discarded needles in the dumpster in the alley beside the restaurant, and there was a puncture wound on Christi's neck."

Hankins looked at his partner. A switch flipped between them. Hankins looked like a man who had seen it all. That came with being on the force in a bigger city like Charleston. He said, "At that point, it became real to Brian. Shelly may have known about Christi and Tommy, but not that Brian was going to kill them. He was going to have them stuffed in the back of the goons' truck and do a switcheroo when he wrecked the RV."

Gomez put her hands on her hips and faced the two captives. "But they only ended up having one body go along for the ride."

"After all, Brian likely paid Dwayne enough money to cover

a string of murders," I said.

"Sounds like this Dwayne is a moron who lacks a conscience?" Hankins said. "Letting these poor people get killed inside his establishment. He's just asking for trouble and time in jail."

"I think he did," I said. "Except that Brian probably didn't tell him what his full plan was until he plunged the needles into their necks."

"I wonder how Dwayne and the goons reacted when Brian did the deed," Graves said rhetorically.

By this point, Brian seemed resigned to his fate. His chin trembled as he stared off into space. Shelly sobbed.

"It was all going according to plan until the murders. He panicked and knew what he was about to put Shelly through to fake their deaths and couldn't do that to her. He went on this redemption tour after leaving her to cleanse his soul or whatever before carrying out his ultimate plan, which he meant to do that night."

There were many threads to grasp for me to tie together. I knew I would leave a few floating about. My brain would only let me explain so much in its current state.

"How did he perpetuate the myth of his death?" Hankins prompted.

"It started with the killings of Christi and Tommy," I said. "Brian killed them both at the same time and must have had second thoughts about carrying out the climax of his plot." I stopped for a moment and considered the needles. "I don't know if Dwayne knew Brian had planned to kill them beforehand. It would depend on if Dwayne supplied the syringes or Brian. If they came from Dwayne, then he had to know Christi and Tommy were going to die." I looked at Gomez. "I'll let you all sort that out."

"Thanks," she said in a wry tone.

I scratched the side of my face and stretched out my legs. "Not wanting to subject Shelly to crashing and setting their RV on fire, Brian left Christi in the cooler and left Dwayne to figure out what to do with her body."

"Why was her body still there?" Hankins asked.

I raised and dropped my shoulders. "By the time Brian made that decision, maybe it was too close to when the Grub N' Go workforce would have come in to prep for the day. Instead of trying to ditch the body elsewhere, Dwayne was stuck with it. They rarely use their freezer anyway, and he stuck a sign on it saying that it was broken and not to open the door. He hoped no one would and took a colossal risk in stashing her body there."

"Clark, being the snoop he is, decided on a whim to open the door when he was there," Gomez said. "Then out dropped the body."

Hankins let out an incredulous chuckle. "Just like that?"

"Just like that," I said. "I opened the door, and she plopped to the floor in front of me, wrapped in butcher's paper."

"That's a big salami," he said.

I forced back a smile. "It was."

Hankins leaned forward in his chair. "Where was Tommy's body during all of this?"

Gomez answered, "With the knuckleheads in their truck."

I spread my hands. "I'm not clear on some details of what happened next, but I think I'm close on most."

Graves tapped the glass. "Where was Shelly during all of this?"

"She was likely in her RV when the murders occurred. I think she's telling the truth there. The next afternoon in the time before the causeway crash, I left her with my parents because I had to tend to my bookstore," I answered. "We were still in that twenty-four-hour period where the police wouldn't open an investigation into Brian's disappearance, so she was in a holding pattern. At least I thought she was until I learned that she never called the police to begin with. Anyway, she had no possessions when I found her. We went to Wal-Mart to get a few things late that night. She told my mom that she arranged for an Uber to pick her up and take her to Target to get something else."

"Like what?"

"Like nothing. My guess is that she sent a message to Brian to pick her up and said he was an Uber driver. When he came to Mom and Dad's house to get her, then they wouldn't have known the difference if they saw the car she hopped into."

"When would this have been?" Hankins said. "How does her leaving your parents' place fit into the timeline?"

"It would have had to have been after the explosion," I said.

He sat back in his seat and re-crossed his arms. "How did that go down and how on Earth did Brian escape it?"

"That was the true moment of Brian's genius," I said.

"Here's how it went down," I said, and kept my eyes on Brian.

He was looking into the mirror to find the person talking. Me.

"By the time I saw him pulling out from the Neighborhood Wal-Mart across from Ocean Lakes, he had accomplished most of his plan and was in close contact with the goon squad toting the body of Tommy Toliver. He had grown a beard, put on a lot of weight, and let his curly hair grow out. But he shaved his hair off after abandoning Shelly. In the last video she uploaded, he had it. Nor was he wearing glasses like he did in every other video.

"When I saw Brian pull up to the stoplight, he looked like a different person. If people ever had reason to go searching for him, they would look at his appearance when he disappeared. When I recognized his RV, it looked like he was wearing a thick black hat. In retrospect, that hat was a bicycle helmet. He was setting himself up to crash in spectacular fashion. I don't know if he had Dwayne scout locations for a crash during prior to their arrival in Myrtle Beach or if he and Shelly went across the Atlantic Avenue causeway during their time in the stay and knew that would be the perfect spot to carry out his plan.

"The causeway bridge comes after a straight stretch of road

where he could pick up enough speed to cut the wheels left and right to cause the camper van to flip. He kept up his crazy behavior by driving erratically through Surfside Beach and Garden City. I tried to keep up as best as I could, but when he cut over into the turn lane to Atlantic Avenue, I lost him and had to circle back. When I got back to Atlantic, I saw his RV swerve and roll over the side of the bridge and into the marsh below."

I raised a finger. "Here is where the magic happened. The two peons had been waiting and motored past the onlookers and pulled to a stop between us and Brian. I was way back in that line and had climbed from my Jeep and ran toward the bridge to help. They got there first. When they got out of their truck, they had Tommy's arms in between them draped around their shoulders so they could carry him over the side. I wondered why someone who looked injured already would try to help, but it all happened so fast that I didn't have time to question it."

"Like a *Weekend at Bernie's* scenario?" Hankins said. I had to give it to him. The man had a macabre sense of humor. He referred to a movie from the late '80s where two men attempted to convince people on an island that their boss was still alive so they could escape suspicion of murder. It was a dark comedy that had its moments.

"Sort of like that." I stood up and tapped the two-way mirror. Now Brian and Shelly knew where to look. I continued, "They jumped over the side of the bridge with Tommy in tow and reached the wrecked RV. Someone popped open the door, which, thankfully for them and Brian, was facing up. They switched out Brian's body for Tommy's and then ignited the spilled gasoline."

Gomez said, "Early indications from the crime scene techs are that the first explosion came from an accelerant, a tank of spare gasoline that got jostled about in the crash. The fire reached the gas tank, which was half-empty so more oxygen would have been inside of it, causing an even bigger explosion. Both happened close together."

"I was standing too close when it happened," I said. "That's how I got banged up."

"Threw him back fifteen feet," Gomez stated.

"Jeez, kid," Hankins said.

"Tell me about it," I said. "They pull the switch with Brian and Tommy and light the fire, climb back to their truck without saying a word to anyone, and speed away. Next thing I knew, I was in a hospital bed."

Hankins's mouth hung open for a moment before asking Gomez, "What happened next?"

"The kids in the truck along with Brian got away before anyone could or would stop them," Gomez said. "All the focus was on the RV and if anyone was inside of it. Fire trucks and police arrived within minutes. By then, Brian and the kids in the truck were long gone. Witnesses gave us descriptions of the young men and their truck as best they could, but if you've spent any time around Myrtle Beach the last few years, then you know a lot of these trucks with the Carolina squat and the people who drive them all look similar."

Hankins looked at me. "And you figured this out. How?"

I nodded at Shelly. "From a few things she let slip and guessed that they would be here today under false identities. I don't know how much of Brian's plan she knew. Like that he planned to kill Christi and Tommy or crash the camper van. All I know was that when he got in touch with her when she was at my parents' place, he must've given her some sort of reasonable explanation, so she followed suit." I sat back down in the chair and got comfortable. Standing for the past minute had caused my back to scream at me.

"On Saturday night at Grub N' Go, after finding the body, she mentioned they were going on a cruise as a last hurrah before going back to his real world. If she was aware of his plan, then that was a grave error on her part."

"I checked the ship manifest," Gomez said, "and neither Brian McConnell nor Shelly Garland were listed."

Hankins leaned to one side. "Which meant he used their new identities to book the cruise."

"Yup," I said. "Gomez let me look at the list. Neither Brian McConnell nor Shelly Garland were on there. I didn't expect them to be."

"What were you looking for?" Hankins asked.

"Their aliases."

"And you found them?"

I smiled and nodded. "I did but didn't know what exactly I was looking for. When I first met Shelly, she mentioned how big of a fan of Food Network's Guy Fieri Brian was. Guy Fieri is not the man's real name. Close, but not quite. I used to watch those shows with my wife. His real name is Guy Ferry. That's the name Brian assumed as his new fake identity. That name was on the list, as was Lori Ferry. The real name of Guy Fieri's wife."

Hankins humphed. "You're saying that Brian wanted to be so much like this guy on TV that he became him?"

"Something like that, yes," I said.

We watched Shelly and Brian stew in the interview room. I hefted myself to my feet and tapped on the glass. Brian looked at where I tapped my finger.

"You almost got away with it, too," I said. "I've never

formally met you, and I hope I never do. I think you dreamed of this grand scheme to escape your life and didn't stop to think about the harm and deaths it would cause. Your hotshot lawyers will try a multitude of defenses to get you off the hook, but we both know you knew exactly what you were doing. Unless she ends up in jail too, I hope Shelly ends up living a happy life. But you," I stopped. My head hurt. My ears hurt. My ribs ached. The rest of my body protested standing up. All because of what that man on the other side of the glass did. I gritted my teeth. "I hope you rot behind bars."

THIRTY-SIX

Several hours later, Gomez and I drove toward Myrtle Beach on 17, through the marshland south of Georgetown. I was hopped on a fresh batch of pain meds and the euphoric rush of catching a killer. Gomez had a similar glow, minus the oxycodone.

Gomez had spent most of the trip with an earbud in her ear, communicating with the Myrtle Beach and Horry County police departments on the phone. I tried to eavesdrop as much as I could, but she said little that I could hear or understand. I resigned myself to watching the scenery flow by out the car window.

Brian had been so dumbfounded that my description of the events matched what happened that he didn't argue. Just sat there with his mouth hanging open. Everyone in the room knew by his body language that he was guilty of the crimes I described. Still, he wouldn't confess to it. He remained adamant that he would wait for his lawyer before saying anything.

They arrested Shelly on suspicion of conspiracy to commit murder but couldn't hold her. The only thing Brian *would* say was that Shelly had nothing to do with it. That didn't stop the police from slapping handcuffs on her for hindering an investigation and accessory after the fact.

We'd left the precinct, and I received a few literal slaps on the back for a job well done. The slaps hurt.

Gomez finally hung up the phone and stared ahead. We were in the middle of a long stretch of straight road as far as the eye could see. Loblolly pines lined both sides of the road in an unbroken line for an eternity. Raindrops dribbled on the windshield. Dark clouds hung in the sky ahead of us.

We were twenty minutes out of Georgetown and a little over an hour from Myrtle Beach. Two innocent young people died to help Brian perpetuate his scheme, and we got him before he disappeared from the world.

"What is going to happen with Brian and Shelly now?" I asked.

"They'll be extradited back to Horry County for arraignment. Brian is going to face several serious charges, including a double homicide. Not to mention reckless endangerment from his Fast and Furious spree through Surfside and Garden City. They'll likely find more misdemeanors to pin on him."

"He should go away for a long time," I said. "What about Shelly? Do you think she knew nothing about all this?"

She raised a sculpted brow. "Do you?"

"I don't see how she couldn't."

"Me neither. That's what she'll say. If Brian backs her up on it, which he will, then the investigators will have to find evidence she did."

"What about phone records from the day she disappeared? Will they be able to get the texts between her and Brian?"

"They should if they exist. That should tell us how much she knew. We should also be able to get the communications between Brian, Shelly, Dwayne, Jules, and Vincent."

"What if Shelly truly knew nothing?"

"Then she'll go free."

After spending two days with the young woman, part of me hoped they were telling the truth, and she was ignorant of the entire scheme so she could go back to Louisiana and live her life. She was bright, friendly, and pleasant. Maybe not the brightest bulb in the box, but a sweet girl.

"Then Brian will plead insanity," I said.

Gomez tilted her chin. "He might try, but he took so many actions that he had previously planned that it won't fly."

"Will he get off easy if he cooperates?"

"I wouldn't say easy," she said, "but the punishment wouldn't be as harsh."

"I think he was in his right mind the entire time. He had this planned out for over a year and almost saw it to its completion."

Gomez laughed.

"What's so funny?" I asked.

"Can you imagine? You've spent all this time, effort, and money trying to escape to another life, almost kill yourself in a staged RV accident, and you can literally see the ultimate goal of your plans, round a corner and there we are. Ready to bust him."

The irony in Brian's outcome was amusing on some level. "He got what he deserved."

"True," she said and reached out with her right hand and grabbed my left one, squeezing it. "He might've gotten away with it if it weren't for you, Clark. You did it again. I, we, can't thank you enough."

Her hand made my blood pressure rise. My heart pounded against broken ribs. I looked at our hands locked together. It was something that I had dreamed of doing since our errant date during the Golden Mile case.

I let go of her hand.

She took her eyes off the road and looked at me when I did.

I finally mustered up the courage to ask what I'd been wanting to ask since after Connor West washed ashore. "What is this with us?"

She blinked. "What is what?"

I intertwined my fingers in hers and held up both hands. "This? These moments of affection we share. Is there something to this, or am I imagining things?"

She turned her attention back to the road and pulled her hand away from mine to steer. Rain came in torrents. A typical Carolina afternoon pop-up thunderstorm. The windshield wipers swiped back and forth as fast as they could but had trouble keeping up. We came upon a Circle K gas station, and she pulled into the lot and parked the car far away from the pumps.

She turned those beautiful green eyes on me. They were misty. Her dark hair fell over one semi-bare shoulder. Blood thundered through my ears. It hurt.

Since knowing her, I had rarely seen this affectionate look in her eyes. Now it was here in full force, and I was jelly in my seat. "Clark."

Here goes. Her next words could change the dynamic of our relationship. For the first time since Autumn's passing, I wanted a romantic connection with someone else. With this woman in front of me. I've seen sides of her she didn't convey in police company. Sensitive and carefree sides. It didn't seem like she had many friends outside of the force, and since she was a transplant from New Jersey and had focused on her career, I imagined she had to bottle up much of this side of her personality to keep up her official bearing.

She placed one hand on the bottom of the steering wheel and caressed the back of her wrist with the other. With a bite of her lip, she looked to the side and wiped away a tear.

"Clark," she said again, "since I've met you, I've relied on you when I shouldn't. Chief Kluttz knows that I've let you get too close to investigations."

"Even when you told me to keep away," I said.

"Yes, even then. Sometimes I would tell you to stay out of it knowing full well you would not listen."

"Sorry."

She ignored me. "And every time, you surprised me. When we met, you were this damaged person. We could all see it. Miss Margaret and Karen cornered me one time and warned me you were fragile, even two years past Autumn's death. You were stuck in a rut and didn't seem inclined to get yourself out of it."

I grinned. "Those two are like having extra grandmas around. Always looking out for me. Always prying into my business."

"That can be good, and I think they're good for you." I nodded in agreement. She continued, "Then you figured out what happened to Paige Whitaker. This closed off person you'd been vanished, and *you* emerged." She reached for my hand. Mine met her halfway. "I saw how much you cared for those who died and tried to find closure for their families. I wrestled with myself for days over whether to tell you my suspicions about Autumn's death, but when I saw how it made you happy to share a moment with Paige's husband, who found himself in a similar situation to what you went through, my heart ached. I'm not supposed to get emotionally involved with cases, suspects, or the people involved in them."

She took the hand off the steering wheel and held it to her

chest. "That touched me. Deeply."

"I understood what he was going through and felt the urge to help."

"And doing what you did took courage. There aren't many like you, Clark. You're a rare breed." She looked both ways to see if anyone was looking, which with us being inside the car, there weren't. "And don't tell my boyfriend I said this, but you're about the most handsome bookstore owner I've ever met."

The air in the car suddenly grew warmer. "You're not so bad yourself."

"Thanks." I didn't like the way this conversation was going. I sensed a big "but" coming after the "boyfriend" reminder.

"The night of the gala at the Chapin Art Museum, my boyfriend and I just had a fight."

This was an area she never spoke about, nor did I ask. If she wanted to tell me what happened with him, I would not press it. I said, "Okay."

"I had to call someone. The evening called for me to have a date. It would have looked bad had I shown up alone. You were the first person I thought of calling to be my arm candy."

"You would have been the first person I would have called had the roles been reversed."

She gave a reassuring smile and went on. "To be honest, I was so mad at him that evening that I left my inhibitions at home."

I cocked an eyebrow. "What do you mean?"

"That I didn't care. I was attracted to you, and I was going to let the night lead me to wherever it went."

"Oh," I said, catching her drift.

"Who knows what would have happened had we not rushed out of the party to go find Cade. You know what took place next."

The sight of Cade Howard laying facedown through the window of his home with a bullet hole in his back haunted me to this day.

"I do." It was my turn to talk. "After Autumn died, I didn't think about finding anyone like her until I met you. Didn't think it was possible. I watched you operate and saw how much you *cared* about getting the bad guy that you would include me when you could. Do you remember the first time I saw you out of uniform?"

She touched a finger to her chin. "Was it at the Bar-B-Cue House in Surfside?"

"It was. That was when I laid out what happened to Paige Whitaker."

"What about it?"

I ran a finger across the dashboard. "It was then that I saw the real you. Not working woman, Gina Gomez. You were wearing a blue jogging outfit and had your hair down. Not gonna lie. You made it difficult for me to string my words together. It struck me that here was this smart, articulate, gorgeous woman sitting beside me, interested in what I had to say."

"Well, yeah, dummy." She smiled. "I was interested because it had to do with catching a killer."

I returned the smile. "True. Then every time I saw you afterward in work attire, I pictured you in that jogging outfit. When we'd talk and sometimes you would touch my arm. It sent shockwaves through my system. It made me notice you differently. I don't know if you were being flirty on purpose or not, but that's the way it seemed to me."

We looked into each other's eyes for a few moments. Rain thundered on the car. It limited the visibility outside to five feet.

"Maybe a little flirty," she admitted, drawing out each word.

Right now, with that look in her eyes and the way I felt, I wanted to do nothing more than wrap her in my arms and fog up the windows on the inside of the car. A small corner of the back of my mind idly wondered if the meds were clouding my judgment here. The other ninety-nine percent of my brain that hadn't been with a woman in so long snuffed that thought from existence.

"I like you," I said in a manner that indicated that "like" was a loose way of putting it.

Her gaze held steady. She took a deep breath. "I like you too, Clark. Maybe as more than friends or working partners or however you want to classify our relationship."

Here it was. I asked, knowing what her answer would be, "But?"

"I'm in a relationship."

When her answer came, it wasn't as deflating as I feared it would be in all the times that I'd imagined this very conversation. I was prepared for the answer. This was a conversation that needed to be had between us. "I realize that."

She bit her lower lip. "And it's serious."

"But?" I asked again, with the hope she'd say more.

"But." She reached out and rubbed my leg. "I feel something for you I'm trying to fight."

"If you're trying to fight it, why make it you and me today? You could have called Moody and asked him to come with us."

Her hand was warm on my leg. "You're right. I could have but didn't want to. I wanted to spend the day with you, Clark. After seeing how vulnerable you were in the hospital the other day because of another crazy escapade made me realize I could have lost you. We don't know each other extremely well, but the thought of you not being around caused this pit in my heart, and I didn't know what I would do if you were gone. I didn't want to fight it."

Tears welled in her eyes again.

I took her hand off my leg and held it in mine. Leaning forward, I said, "Then why fight it?"

She met me halfway and put an arm over my shoulder and around my neck. I placed a hand on her side. It felt good and firm and warm. The fabric of her tank top had a satiny quality to the touch.

Her arm drew me closer. My eyes closed. Our lips met. Hers were pillowy and moist and everything I envisioned they would be. Everything around me went blurry as we kissed. At least in my world, it did.

All the pent-up emotions we had for each other exploded in a furious sequence of caressing and tongue gymnastics. Three years of loneliness melted away in an instant when she lunged across the divide between the seats, pinning me against the door. I gasped and ignored the pain. One of my hands embraced the back of her head while the other rubbed the small of her back. Soft hands cradled my chin.

Raindrops pounded the fogging windows. We were oblivious to a world outside the Camry.

She took her hands off my face, but kept her lips locked on mine. I hooked a finger around the strap of her tank top. She reached down and grabbed the hem of my shirt. Our lips parted. We had to come up for air. We stared at each other as we caught our collective breath. Her chest heaved with each gasp. Mine did too.

She closed her eyes and took a deep breath. A large tear

poured over the bottom of her right eye and fell down her cheek. That perfect cheek I wanted to hold in my hands and wipe away the tear.

Then she did the last thing I ever expected every time I imagined this conversation and that result.

She reached into her pocket and withdrew something small. She held it for me to see between two fingers.

"I've tried to fight my attraction to you because of this," she said.

She was holding an engagement ring.

CHAPTER
THIRTY-SEVEN

It was a quiet ride back to my home in Surfside Beach. The mix of affection and lust that I had when she showed me the engagement ring dissipated into nothingness. I might have gotten out of her car and walked home if we hadn't been in the middle of nowhere, in an absolute downpour, with a battered and bruised body.

The sensible part of me won out, but after she explained that her boyfriend, now fiancé, proposed to her last weekend, I had nothing to say. She talked some and apologized for leading me on like she did, but I didn't want to respond.

What I needed was time to think and process my feelings. My actions and words now could echo for eternity, and I didn't want to ruin what we had. Whatever remained.

The rain had stopped north of Pawleys Island. Night had fallen. She dropped me off at my house, where she apologized again. She had to go to police headquarters. My part in the double murder investigation was done. Thank goodness.

I almost said nothing. Almost. After climbing from the car, I stood in place with my hand resting on top of the open car door, looking out on the lake behind my house. Frogs croaked in chorus. Bats fluttered in the streetlights lining the street, chasing bugs. Puddles remained from the earlier storms. Water reflected in the lights. A soft breeze brushed against my skin.

After summoning the courage, I bent down and looked in the car at Gomez. The interior car light illuminated her. One hand on the wheel. The other poised on the gear shifter. Her eyes were on me. Those beautiful green eyes.

"We both know what happened back there in that gas station parking lot," I said. "You can't ignore it. Neither can I, but you put me in a difficult position. It's not fair to me. You also didn't wear that ring in your pocket today for a reason. You didn't want me to know about your engagement. Go home, sort out your feelings, speak with your fiancé. Whatever. Figure it out and let me know. Or not. Whichever you prefer."

"I will," she breathed.

I nodded at the front of the house. "I'll be here if you want me."

After closing the car door, I limped to the porch. The beams of her headlights lit up the front of the house so I could see to unlock the door. I cracked it open and turned and waved to let her know I could get in.

Her car didn't move.

The driver's side door opened.

Her left foot hit the ground and stayed.

My heart leapt in my throat. Despite the engagement ring, I envisioned her climbing from the car and running into my arms before we entered the house together, locked the door, and closed the blinds.

Perhaps she had the same thought, which was why she lingered.

None of that happened. Without a word, she pulled her left

leg back inside the car, closed the door, backed the Camry out of the driveway, and disappeared into the night.

* * *

Alcohol and oxycodone don't mix. I left the bottle of Woodford Reserve on top of the fridge untouched, as much as it tempted me.

I couldn't sleep, even after taking sleeping pills. The thought of them not mixing with the oxy never crossed my mind.

I felt sorry for Shelly. We may never know how much she was aware of Brian's scheme. If she was ignorant of it, then she'd wasted the last year of her life while Brian plotted to carry out his plan. Of course, the experience of traveling around the country the way they did was something that I'd dreamed of doing. Autumn and I had talked about buying an RV and driving around the country, visiting all the national parks.

We were going to wait until retirement to do so.

Something kept me up. Was it possible it had been Shelly's idea to break away from their lives to begin with? Maybe she saw the effects the career had on Brian's dad and didn't want that for him. What if she was in on it from the start and Brian reconsidered endangering her at the last minute?

I may never know the answers to those questions.

One question I think I knew the answer to was what would have happened today had Gina not had that ring in her pocket?

That moment in her car got steamy. The windows fogged. It didn't take much.

But she was engaged. I still hadn't met her fiancé, but that didn't matter. My morals didn't allow for me to get between her and her man, no matter how attracted I was to her. If she was that committed, I would not try to get her to break that commitment.

It was against all that I found good and proper.

I went to sleep sometime before dawn, wondering where I would have fallen asleep if it weren't for that ring.

CHAPTER
THIRTY-EIGHT

Gomez remained true to her word. She sent me a text message with Banner's wife's information. Beyond that, I didn't see or hear hide nor hair of Gina Gomez over the next few weeks.

I called the wife. Her name was Brenda. I told her who I was and why I was calling. She said she remembered me and the case and invited me to her home for coffee. I wasn't about to pass that up.

She lived in the Del Webb community along the 17 Bypass. Her house overlooked the Intracoastal Waterway. It was a charming brick ranch home with green shutters and a matching tin roof. The landscaping out front was clean and well-kept. I pulled into her driveway, parked the Jeep, and walked to the front porch, where I rang the doorbell.

A glass storm door with a palmetto tree etched into it fronted a solid green door painted to match the shutters and roof. The green door opened, and woman of average height and bulk appeared. She had short, tightly curled hair covered by a visor cap. Her face was smooth apart from crow's feet at the corners of her eyes. A pair of thick eyeglasses rested on an angular nose.

Her smile was warm and inviting. She pushed open the glass door. "You must be Clark. Come on in."

"Thank you so much for having me," I said, stepping through

the door and into a tall entryway. The home smelled of herbs, baked chicken, and coffee. My stomach growled.

The house had an open floor plan with a tall ceiling, giving it the feeling of being bigger than it was. From the foyer, a door to the garage stood on my right, and doors to three rooms — likely a bathroom and bedrooms — lined one wall to my left. A granite-covered kitchen with stainless steel appliances and tile backsplash was in the corner at the front of the house beside a dining room. Another open doorway lay beyond that, peeking in at a master bedroom. A charming living room suite and a flat panel TV took up the middle of the open space.

One wall contained pictures of Ed Banner. At least, I assumed it was him. I'd never seen a picture of him until now. I took it to be a memorial wall. It housed family photos and pictures of him as a member of the police department. One photo of him had to be from early in his career. It showed him in full dress uniform with a gawky smile on his face. Others showed him with various police and government officials, often shaking hands with someone. Those pictures were like the ones I had taken when I received a commendation from Mayor Sid Rosen. He appeared in a few of the pictures.

Large windows lined the back of the home, providing grand views of a covered porch and the Intracoastal below. A sailboat cruised past while I followed Brenda to the kitchen.

"You'll have to forgive my mess," she said, waving a hand at dirty pots and pans crowded in the sink. "I'm making food for a church potluck we're having tomorrow and haven't cleaned up yet."

"Oh, you don't have to apologize to me," I said. "You should see my kitchen."

My kitchen stayed clean, but I didn't need to mention that.

She led me to a Cuisinart coffee maker that held a full pot of coffee in a glass carafe. A tray of fresh-baked chocolate chip cookies lay beside it with a stack of cocktail napkins. The chocolate chips were still gooey and had a bit of sheen. Fresh ones. A bag of Gevalia coffee sat behind the machine against the wall. It had a nutty aroma. I wouldn't turn my nose up at it.

She reached into the fridge and withdrew a tall carton of half-and-half and set it on the counter beside the mugs. A spoon and a container of sugar lay beside that. It was a tidy setup.

"I appreciate this," I said. "The coffee smells wonderful."

"Thanks," she said. "Don't forget those cookies. Used my Nanna's recipe."

"Looks delicious."

After filling a mug with coffee and stacking two generously proportioned cookies on top of a napkin, she led me to a covered porch at the rear of the house. An unseasonal cool breeze blew along the waterway. A thick, briny scent touched my nose. Thank goodness for the coffee and cookies.

We sat down at a bistro table with three iron chairs. Ones that wouldn't get blown about in a hurricane. A black, wrought-iron fence ran the length of her property along the bank of the waterway. Neatly trimmed grass in a thin strip and a persimmon tree in the corner gave Brenda's backyard a sense of coziness.

"This is nice," I said as we got comfortable.

"Thank you," Brenda responded. "Eddie used to sit out here and sip his herbal teas and read the paper in the mornings before heading down to the precinct. I'd drink my coffee and scroll through Instagram."

"Sounds a little like Autumn and me. Our house sits on a

lake in Surfside. We'd sit on our back deck in the mornings. I'd drink coffee and watch the water. She'd drink tea and read a book."

"That sounds nice. You sound like you miss her."

I took a sip of coffee. It was a notch below scalding hot. Just the way I liked it. "Every day."

She held her cup in both hands and watched another boat cruise by. She had a northern accent. Vermont maybe. "It gets easier, doesn't it?"

Here was a woman who lost her husband three months after Autumn's death. We had both spent almost the same amount of time coping with our losses. If anyone understood how it felt, it would be her.

"Eventually," I conceded.

"Have you been able to move on?"

My mind flashed back to Gomez pinning me against the door of her car. A thought I'd had many times since that day. A thought that I tried to hold back but couldn't. "Not quite, but I'm ready. How about you?"

"Good," she said. "I don't know that I ever will, to tell the truth. Eddie and I had been married for over forty years. He would have retired a year after his death."

"I'm so sorry."

She batted a hand in my direction. "Don't mention it."

I didn't. "How did he die again? Heart attack?"

"Yup." She sipped from the mug and pointed over to a bare corner of the porch. One side of the patio was free of decoration or chairs. "Died right over there while reading the paper and drinking his tea. I'd gone inside to get a refill. When I came back out, he was slouched over in his chair. Dead as a doornail."

The hair stood up on the back of my neck. My mind tried to tie separate strings together on the fly, but the connection wasn't forming at the moment. "Just like that?"

"Yup. Just like that."

"Makes you appreciate being alive."

"That it does. We were going to sell this house and move to Florida after he left the job. We'd already told the kids. Prepared them."

"How many kids do you have?"

"Three. They all live around here. You have any kids?"

"Unfortunately, not. Not for lack of trying, though."

She laughed and nodded. "That's the fun part."

We were quiet for a moment. A pair of seagulls went squawking by. It was a pleasant morning, and I was thankful to be alive after what happened on the causeway. My injuries had healed, as had my ears. Besides a few extra pains in the morning when getting out of bed, I felt close to normal.

"I understand you have some questions for me," Brenda said. "I'm not sure what I can tell you, but I'm more than happy to help."

"I can't tell you how much I appreciate this."

She put her hand on top of mine and squeezed. "Don't mention it."

"Thanks."

She turned to face me. Her expression turned serious. "No. I mean it. Don't mention that we had this conversation."

The hair stood up on the back of my neck. "Why do you say that?"

"Let's just say that there was some bad voodoo going on around the time of Eddie's death."

"What kind of bad voodoo?"

"It's best I only tell you what you need to know."

"What do you know? What happened the night Autumn died?"

"I don't know. Eddie didn't talk about it."

If Banner said nothing to her, then I wasn't sure how fruitful this conversation would be. Another dead-end most likely. "Then why do you say there was some bad voodoo going on?"

She cocked her head and considered. "Now, that's not true. It wasn't all bad voodoo. Some strange things happened he told me to keep quiet about."

"What kind of strange things?"

She bit into a cookie. Strings of melted chocolate fell over her fingers. She licked it off. That reminded me I had two of them on a napkin and took a bite of my own. Reminded me of my mom's cookies.

"I tended to our bills and whatnot. Made sure the checking account stayed in the positive. About a week after your wife died, I checked our bank statement. It showed a fifty-thousand-dollar deposit made from a bank in Grand Cayman."

I almost choked on my coffee. "Fifty K?"

"Yup. I told Eddie. He told me to move it to another account ASAP."

"Did he say how the money got there?"

"He told me to not ask questions."

"Did you?"

Her eyes narrowed. "He spent thirty-five years on the force. Most of that as a detective. During the early 90s, he got involved in a case that almost got him killed. He shot two men during the investigation. They died. He lived. He was put on administrative duty, confined to a desk. Never told me about the men he shot, nor was it reported in the news. He couldn't talk about it."

"What do you think happened?"

"I hate to say it, but I think someone had something on Eddie that they could use to get him in trouble."

"Like, illegal activity?"

"That's what I always thought." She took another bite of her cookie. "Don't ask. Don't tell. I'd like to tell you that Eddie was an honest cop, but I can't. He kept some of what he did to himself."

"He operated in the gray?"

"What do you mean?"

"Like, there's right and wrong. Laws. Good and bad. It sounds like your husband was good at his job, at least from what Detectives Gomez and Moody told me."

"That old goat still around? Moody?"

"Still hanging in there."

"He's gotta be getting near retirement."

"Close," I said.

She laughed. "He was Eddie's partner for a while. The man doesn't have a lot of gray matter that works, but now and then, he'd surprise Eddie with some epiphany that let them solve a case."

"Been my experience, too."

"That's what I've been told."

That got my attention. "You've been talking about me with others?"

"Sure have. I wouldn't have let you into my home otherwise."

"Who did you speak with about me?"

"Gina Gomez."

"Oh?"

"Yeah. She had nothing but good things to say about you. Explained the situation you were in with Autumn and trying to figure out what happened. I want to help."

That Gomez would still speak well of me spoke volumes about the type of person she was. Although she never told me how the conversation went with her fiancé—leading me to believe that she was going to remain engaged—she still wanted to help. The anger I had for her lessened with this knowledge.

I said, "On the night of Autumn's death, she said your husband had her go with him to the courthouse."

"Yes, that was protocol. Always have two to investigate a death."

"Right. She said he treated her like a rookie and had her stay at the outer fringes of Autumn's office while he investigated."

"Sounds about right. Eddie wasn't too keen on the younger people on the force."

"Gomez said that evening, he took several phone calls where he said little and mostly listened. She said he didn't say much. Any clue who he could have been talking to?"

Her head rocked back and forth on her neck. "Could have been dispatch. Could have been his sergeant."

"Gomez made it sound like it was neither. She found the calls suspicious."

"They weren't made to me. Hmm." She put an elbow on the table and rested that hand on her chin.

"What is it?"

She pushed the chair back and stood. "Hold that thought. Be right back."

I finished my coffee as I watched her go through the French doors and disappear inside the home. A few minutes passed as

I enjoyed the comfortable weather. What had Banner been up to?

She returned, holding two sheets of paper. A blue AT&T logo was at the top of both pages, followed by rows of numbers and words. She set the sheets on the table and explained. "Even though Eddie operated in the gray, he kept meticulous records. He wanted to cover himself if push came to shove."

"Did it ever?"

"More than I can tell you." She flipped the top page over and laid it beside the bottom one. "He kept every cell phone record he could from the time he first started carrying one in the late-90s. They were all locked away in a filing cabinet in the office."

"Have you ever gone through his filing cabinets?"

Her eyebrows arched. "Do I look like I want to open Pandora's Box? Never touched them. Left them where they were until today. There was so much dust in that office that I had a coughing fit trying to go through the cabinet doors."

"I'm sorry."

"Again, don't mention it. You apologize too much."

I almost said I was sorry again but abstained. "Yes, ma'am."

"Better." She tapped one sheet. "Anyway. He labeled all the cabinet drawers, so it was easy to find the phone records from that month. It was one of the last ones he ever received, which made finding them even easier."

I looked down at the pages. They might as well glowed like they were made of gold. I hoped it wasn't fool's gold.

"Do you mind?"

She leaned aside so I could get access to the phone records. "Of course not."

"Thank you."

I reached for the first page. It listed the phone number and charges associated with that phone line. Looked like Banner had a good deal on his service.

The other page was the important one. The call logs. Four columns listed the time, date, phone number, and duration of the calls.

I ran my finger down the list and came to the date of Autumn's death. March 23rd. I counted more than a dozen calls from that day. I recognized Gomez and Moody's numbers on the list. As my finger moved down to the time of evening when Banner would have been investigating Autumn, it froze.

Three phone numbers repeated themselves. One call lasted a minute and fifteen seconds. The next call lasted fifty-three seconds. The third and last call was ten seconds long.

I recognized the phone number too. It was emblazoned upon my brain.

It was the same unlisted phone number that sent the threatening text messages to Autumn the night before her death.

CHAPTER
THIRTY-NINE

I went to my safe place. The bookstore. I didn't work. I just wanted to be there. I sat in the same chair near the window where Andrea and I talked the day after the explosion. She came in most days to get tea. We'd chat for a few minutes each time before she went back to her shop next door.

She and Karen had hit it off to where Andrea's daughter, Libby, would come in and play "bookstore worker" with Karen behind the counter. It was cute. Karen had even babysat Libby a few times so Andrea could work late. It helped to create a support network.

Moody told me that Dwayne rolled over on Brian. The owner of Grub N' Go was in serious jeopardy as an accomplice to Brian's crimes, but in telling everything that went on in Brian's scheme, corroborated by Tweedle Dee and Tweedle Dum, they faced a reduced sentence down the road when they faced a judge.

He said that Brian had contacted him and wanted his help in leaving the country and that he would pay Dwayne a significant amount of money to do so. It fell through the grapevine that the amount Brian paid Dwayne was a cool half million dollars. Enough to pay the Goobers to keep quiet and get Brian and Shelly what they needed to start another life.

Brian awaited trial behind bars. They deemed him too much of a flight risk to be released on bond. Go figure.

They charged him with two counts of murder, conspiracy to defraud the government, faking his death, fraud, reckless endangerment, and vehicular assault.

He refused to implicate Shelly in the mess. Dwayne didn't include her either. He said that Brian wanted to leave her out of it until they were on the cruise ship and bound for the Bahamas. They released her of her own recognizance, and she went home to Louisiana.

We'll never know how much she actually knew of Brian's plot. She will testify at trial, but no one knew at this point what or if she would say anything implicating herself in the plot.

She may have been ignorant of the entire mess. I hoped she was.

I hadn't spoken to Gomez since she dropped me off at the house the night we came back from Charleston. The contact information she sent me about Brenda Banner came via text message.

No matter how much I tried to get Gina out of my mind, I spent many a lonely night since then thinking about her and what might have been. There was nothing I would morally do about it. I wasn't about to try and break up an engagement. The ball was in her court. It looked like it would remain there.

I'd had writer's block since the causeway incident as well. Hadn't written a word of another book. My agent called me once a week, demanding a progress report. The publisher had set a late-fall deadline to have the next manuscript turned in to them. It would be a struggle to accomplish that. I didn't know what would happen if writer's block stuck.

Progress on the second location of my bookstore in Garden City had stalled out as well. Officials dragged their feet in granting various permits. The supply chain to get the materials I needed to spruce up the interior ground to a halt. Even if the red tape was completed, my contractor couldn't get the supplies he needed to refurbish the interior of the new spot. Meanwhile, I had to pay rent on it every month.

Not much had gone well since I met Shelly Garland. Trips to the liquor store increased as well. Like they had after Autumn's death.

What I needed was something to go right. Something to give me hope. The clock on the wall read thirty minutes until noon.

The store was busy. Winona and Karen hustled while helping customers.

Then an idea struck that lifted my spirits.

I got up and found Karen behind the coffee bar, pouring two cups of coffee for a pair of tourists. After she took care of them, she smiled at me.

"Clark, what's up?"

I flashed a rare smile these days and asked her to do me a favor.

* * *

I went next door to Coastal Décor and opened the door. A bell jingled as I entered. The store contained a tasteful collection of regional furniture and decorations straight from a magazine spread. The store smelled like cinnamon and pears.

No one was inside except for Andrea and Libby. The little girl played on the floor in the middle of the store with a set of dolls, giving them voices and having them carry on conversations amongst themselves. Andrea watched from an Adirondack chair while flipping through a catalog. Her skin had tanned over the past few weeks, making the freckles on her cheeks stand out more. She wore a purple V-neck shirt, a pair of light blue jeans, with a pair of sandals. Her hair was styled the way it was the first day I met her, with two strands of blonde hair hovering over her face and the rest braided along the back of her neck. Dang near perfect.

They looked up as I entered.

"Clark!" Libby shouted, jumped up, ran to me, and gave me a big hug.

"Hey, girl," I said. "What are you playing?"

"Dolls," she replied. "They're getting ready to go shopping."

"Yeah," Andrea said, "they're going to pretend to go to the Coastal Grand Mall and go on a shopping spree."

"Fun," I said.

"Yeah!" Libby grinned. "Want to play?"

"I'm sorry. Maybe a little later." I kneeled to get down to Libby's eye level. "Hey, Karen is working at the bookstore. Do you think you and your dolls might want to go shopping there instead?"

She looked from me to her mom to the dolls. "Yeah! They need new books. Can I Mom? Huh? Can I? Can I?"

"If it's alright with Karen, I guess so," Andrea said, closing the catalog.

"Have you had lunch, Libby?" I asked and straightened my knees.

"Uh-huh. Mom gave me a peanut butter and banana sandwich and applesauce already."

Andrea looked up at me from her chair. "Yeah, the little bugger had an early breakfast and needed an early lunch." She got to her feet and gave me a querying look. "What are you up to?"

I stepped toward her. "Are you hungry? There is a great Venezuelan restaurant named La Vino Tinto near the Chapin Library. I got a hankering for some ceviche. Can you close up shop here for a bit and go for lunch?"

The two of us stood at the same height. Andrea took a step closer and tucked a strand of hair behind her ear. She grinned and said, "I thought you'd never ask."

To be continued...

All books in the series are available on Amazon, Barnes and Noble, Books-a-Million, and wherever books are sold. Don't see them in your local store or library? Ask the bookseller or librarian to order them for you.

Learn more on his website at calebwygal.com.

ACKNOWLEDGEMENTS

Writing a book by its very nature is a lonely endeavor. A writer spends countless hours staring at a computer screen while building stories and worlds. That being said, this writer does need help along the way. As with previous books in this series, I bugged Dr. Stephanie Rose during the day and evening for medical input. More so in this book than the others. I wanted to figure out what would kill Clark and dial it back a little so he could finish this story. Credit goes to her for keeping him alive. Another person who I asked endless questions of is retired police officer Mike Dame (who made an appearance in this book). He helped me with procedural elements throughout and criminal aspects involved in Brian's scheme. As this is a work of fiction, I use literary license and play loose by the rules when it helps to propel the story. In short: don't try this at home.

I would like to thank my editor, Lisa Borne Graves, and alpha readers for helping shape this story. Angie Barnhardt gets credit for naming three of the characters in this book: Shelly Garland, Brian McConnell, and Dwayne Clayton.

Thank you to my readers for your kind words and encouragement.

As always, all mistakes are mine.

ABOUT THE AUTHOR

Caleb is a member of the International Thriller Writers and Southeastern Writers Association, the author of seven novels, social media marketer, woodworker, occasional golfer, reacher of things on high shelves, beach walker, shark tooth finder, and munchkin wrangler.

His two Lucas Caine Adventure novels, *Blackbeard's Lost Treasure* and *The Search for the Fountain of Youth*, were both Semi-Finalists for the Clive Cussler Adventure Awards Competition.

He is currently at work on the next book in the Myrtle Beach Mystery Series.

He lives in Myrtle Beach with his wife and son (the munchkin).

Visit Caleb online at
www.CalebWygal.com

*If you enjoyed this story please
consider reviewing it online and at Goodreads,
and recommending it to family and friends.*